INSTIGATED

MAYA DANIELS

VINCI
BOOKS

By Maya Daniels

Daywalker Series

Investigated

Infiltrated

Instigated

Initiated

Infuriated

Ignited

Vinci Books

vinci-books.com

Published by Vinci Books Ltd in 2026

1

The EU GPSR authorised representative is Logos Europe, 9 rue Nicolas
Poussion, 17000 La Rochelle, France
contact@logoseurope.eu

Chapter One

My nails dig into the mortar between the bricks where I'm clinging for dear life, making my fingers ache. The tips of my boots scrape between bricks, searching for purchase just as a fat drop of rain splatters on the tip of my nose on my upturned face, spraying my eyes. Blinking fast to clear my vision, I finally find one brick protruding from the others, letting the tip of the boot rest there as I press my face to the wall.

"This was a very dumb idea." Huffing under my breath, I try to slow my breathing.

I'm suspended two stories up on the outside of the academy building, hanging for all to see like an idiot. I'm counting on no one looking up, but if I don't move fast I'll eventually be spotted. My arms and legs burn from the effort it takes me to crawl up like a spider in the middle of the night. Hopefully it'll pay off, if my guess is right. With one last slow breath, my heart galloping in my chest, I continue the laborious climb. I've seen humans doing this for fun on TV. Rock climbing they call it, the idiots. Who would do this for fun?

Sweat trickles from between my shoulder blades down my spine by the time I see the curving rooftiles within reach. I can't feel my fingers anymore, and my muscles scream in pain all over my body. Maybe I should do more than just the calming yoga exercises I've been sticking with the last couple of years. I almost laugh at the thought, but I'm too tired. Running for your life is exercise enough, right?

Summoning all the energy I have left, I swing my lower body like a pendulum, arms shaking from the weight as I fling one leg over the edge of the rooftiles. Everything around me swims, dizziness making me lightheaded when I end up hanging with my head down, my braid like a rope tapping the wall. Wedging my foot between the tile and a pipe, I pull my other leg up and finally plop on my back.

Another fat drop of rain splatters my cheek.

Keeping my eyes closed, I take slow, deep breaths, grinding my teeth with the effort to move my hands, which are cramped like claws with my fingers curled from over an hour of gripping bricks. My heart leaps in my throat when a howl breaks the silence. It's answered by the hoot of an owl a moment later. The echoes of the sounds keep me company while I try to catch my breath and kick my butt into gear to get moving. More raindrops pepper my face and I roll to my belly before lifting up on all fours.

They keep an eye on me wherever I go inside the academy. This is the only way I can think of to follow the demon guards I've seen sneaking around. They all go up the wide stairways past the third floor disappearing from view. When I try to follow, a few of them get in my face and I have to fight them if I want to see where they are going. Making a quick decision, I back away from the fight—yeah, I know I was surprised as well—and this is what I come up with as an alternative. Climbing walls Spiderman style like an idiot.

Snorting at my stupidity, I get on my feet and look around the rooftop. The moon casts her silvery glow, breaking apart the shadows. There must be a way to get to this roof from the inside. The tiles look new, the dark gray color not faded or cracked. Either someone is maintaining them or they just use magic. Throwing a glance down to the pebbled path circling the building, my stomach drops in a free-style flip flop. If it's magic, I'm screwed. No way I'm climbing back down the way I came. I'll just sit here until someone finds me. I'll say I am sleepwalking, or something. I'm sure that will go as well as trying to pet a snake.

Rolling my shoulders to release the tension, I shake out my hands and hunch down, creeping closer to the other side of the roof. Stepping lightly on the angled tiles to not make a sound, I get as close to the edge as I can. A hum disturbing the air freezes my movements. Holding my breath and straining my ears, I inch closer, noticing for the first time a raised frame just to the left of where I'm crouched. It's either a door or a window but I couldn't care less. I feel like crying from excitement that I will eventually get out of here like a normal person and not a thief. The hum is slightly louder the closer I get, two distinct voices ringing clear in it. I can't make out any words yet, the darkened window reason enough for the sounds to be muffled. Pressing my knees on the hard tiles, hands braced on the frame on either side, I lean in as close as I dare without pressing my ear on the glass.

"What are we doing?"

Swallowing the scream that lodges in my throat at the hushed whisper next to my ear, my fist connects to a warm, unforgiving palm. Thick fingers wrap around my knuckles a second before my body tilts sideways, gravity pulling it straight toward the window. My eyes scrunch up as I brace for the impact. A muscular arm snakes around my waist, yanking me back into a broad chest and the scent of rainforests and rain fills my nostrils. Clenching my jaw, I beg the fates for patience.

"This is how you get killed." Hissing under my breath, I open my eyes to glare at Fenrir.

"You were really sneaky, so I figured we need to be quiet." Placing me gently next to him and off his lap, the Fae leans over the window like he can see through the dark glass.

"I was sneaky so you wouldn't follow me around." Pushing the words out, I try my best not to yell at him. He tilts his face my way lifting one eyebrow in an unspoken question, *"How did that work out for you?"*

"How did you get here, Fenrir?" He doesn't look one bit tired, his hair smooth as silk while my braid looks like dogs have been gnawing on it while stray hairs stick to the sides of my face.

Not turning, he points behind him and I follow the direction of that one graceful finger to a small trap door gaping open a few feet behind us. I didn't even see it there. It takes everything in me not to whack him across the head, my body screaming at me in pain from the climb.

"What are we looking for here?" Murmuring under his breath, he tilts his head this way and that as if trying to catch a stray word through the thick glass. "Who's down there?"

"We were not looking for anything." Shoving him away with my shoulder, I kneel where I was before he came along. "I, on the other hand, was trying to see why the demons were sneaking up to the top floors and not letting anyone follow."

Eyeing the window frame, I trace my fingers around it to search for a latch, or anything really that will help me open it. Fenrir grunts something I don't hear, blowing a frustrated breath through his nose. It's funny now how I stupidly think I'll do anything without the Fae knowing about it.

"Let me see." After watching me for long moments, he pushes my hands away and nudges me out of my place. "I'm not sure these windows were meant to be opened." His lips barely move with the huffed words, a line forming between his eyebrows.

Chewing on my bottom lip, I glance from Fenrir to the open trap door and back. My body coils up and all my muscles stiffen, ready to spring into action. The Fae is fast, but I am faster. I can get through it and lock him out here if I time it right.

"I wouldn't do that if you don't want the demons to know you've been following them." Not looking away from his task, his tone is so soft I actually have to lean forward to hear his words. "If you lock me out, I'll break this window and catch you before you step foot out of the attic." An arrogant grin stretches his lips when he looks up. "Don't be so surprised, Hellion. I've watched you long enough to anticipate your actions."

"That's because you have stalker tendencies." Blowing out a breath, I keep my eyes locked on his, my mind spinning with ideas. No way I'm getting rid of him tonight. "Can you open it or not?" I sound snappy but the frustration is more from being unable to shake him off than anything else.

Without looking away, Fenrir's hands keep moving,

tracing the frame inside and out. A slow smile replaces the concentration on his face just as I hear the soft click. He winks at me before squeezing his fingers into the tiny gap and pulling the window silently open.

I stick my tongue out at him, which only widens his grin.

"… regardless of what you say. I think the timing is right," a deep voice grumbles from beneath us, pushing all other thoughts out of my head. I lean eagerly forward to hear better. "With all the shit going on, no one will be paying attention to us."

"I dunno about that," another one answers, followed by the shuffling of feet. "It might look like Alexius has the upper hand, but I wouldn't bet against Zoltan unless I see his head separated from his body. Do you really want to be the one standing in front of him answering why the book is missing if he survives?"

"You saw Zoltan led like a dog through the portal, yet here you are still afraid of him. I should've known you were a coward. I'll do it myself," the first demon snarls.

Fenrir snatches my arm to hold me in place. I'm not even aware I lift off my knees to jump down and kill the asshole for calling Zoltan a dog. Fury burns through my chest, my whole body trembling with the effort it takes to stay still. The Fae keeps his firm grip on my arm, but the look on his face is calm and collected.

"You are a fool." The voice of the second demon pulls me out of my murderous thoughts. "Don't look at me like that. You are an idiot if you think Zoltan is the only one you should be afraid of. Argoz and Fenrir will have your head if you get caught, as well as Astara. I don't even want to think what the half-blood will do."

My eyebrows crawl up my forehead all the way to my hairline. Fenrir's arm shakes slightly where he still holds me back, so I grab his wrist to prevent him from pouncing on the demons. I guess hearing them call me a half blood makes him upset. But then his shoulders start shaking too, so I angle myself to get a better look at his downturned face. The jerk is trying incredibly hard not to laugh. As if they have their own mind, my hands shoot out so I can punch the humor off his face. My finger bumps the slightly-opened window, my nail catching on a splinter of the weather-worn wood. The sharp piece stabs underneath my nail bed, crippling me in pain.

I grind my teeth.

"Did you hear that?" The second demon sounds alarmed, so I bite my lip even harder to ensure I don't scream, my eyes crossing from the throbbing of my finger.

"You really are a coward. First, a captured Daywalker makes you shake in fear, then a fucking girl scares you, and now even birds freak you out. You are a disgrace," the first demon spits angrily. "I'll get the book tomorrow night. Alexius is sending someone to pick it up in two days' time. You can explain then why you were sitting on your ass when everything we've ever wanted is within reach."

A door slams, and I jump out of my skin from the loud crash while Fenrir searches my face in concern. Swallowing the bile in my throat, I shove my forefinger in his face. Flinching, he rears back, his eyes crossing when he tries to see what I'm showing him. A tiny, sharp splinter is sticking out from under my short, blunt nail, the bigger part of it embedded in the nail bed. Tears gather at the corners of my eyes. The second demon mutters something intangible before we hear the door open and close again.

Fenrir folds his lips inward, biting on them hard.

My eyes narrow to slits.

"Let me see." Clearing his throat, he tries and fails to keep a straight face while reaching for my hand.

I say nothing when he takes my fingers in his, pinching the splinter between his thumb and forefinger. Clenching my jaw, I squeeze my eyes shut when he yanks it out. Another sharp pain stabs through me from the now-bleeding puncture, this one spearing all the way to my shoulder.

"I believe the humans call this instant karma." Holding the offending splinter like a trophy between us, the jerk grins so wide it looks like his face will split from it.

I punch him.

Sprawling on his back on the rooftiles, the Fae roars with laughter. His hair escapes the rubber band holding it at the base of his neck, the platinum strands contrasting against the dark gray tiles. Head thrown back, I watch his chest shake, the moon casting shadows and sharpening the line of his cheekbones. A snort escapes me when I shake my head at his antics.

He laughs harder, slapping his thigh with one large hand, and his eyes glitter with tears when he looks at me. It's been a long time since I've seen Fenrir laugh and the knot in my chest loosens at the sight. Plopping on my ass next to him, I giggle.

"It hurts like a bitch." Peeking at my nail, I can't see anything other than blood pooling under it.

"I should frame it." Still chuckling, Fenrir sits up holding the stupid splinter like his life depends on it. "Nothing can make agent Drake blink an eye, but this splinter made her almost pass out."

"You are such a jerk. I did not almost pass out." Shoving him away by the shoulder, my eyes drift back to the slightly-opened window. "We have a lead, Fenrir."

He locks his gaze on mine, the too-blue color of his eyes looking as silver as the giant orb in the sky matching the moonlight. All the humor is gone as we stare at each other. It's been days since Roberti took Zoltan and we did nothing but chase our tails the entire time. We have no idea where to look, what to look for, or who to ask.

Myst, the strange female I met when I crossed the portal to the human world, disappeared after the hunters that night and I haven't heard anything from her either. Despair is eating a hole inside me as I think about what may be happening to Zoltan all while I sit here doing nothing. I've been avoiding Astara as well, because I can't look at her. I'm too afraid I'll see disgust and betrayal in her gaze.

Until now.

"I'll tell Argoz…"

"Don't you dare say a word to anyone." Hissing at him, I take a fistful of his shirt and yank his face to mine. His eyes widen comically. 'No one hears about this; do you understand me? I will wait in the library to see what book Alexius needs. If he needs it, I want it more. The demon will lead us to his contact and that will take us to Zoltan. If you screw this up with your rules or whatever, I'll skin you, Fae."

"I was only suggesting a backup, Francesca." Lifting both hands in surrender, he frowns at me. "I want to find him as much as you do, but we don't know who this contact is. You can't help Zoltan if you are dead, or taken away just like him."

"You can come." My hand twists his shirt tighter. "No one else Fenrir. I'm not planning to engage; I'm going to follow."

"Even through the portal." He searches my eyes as understanding dawns on him. "You think they'll lead you to

Zoltan. It's a risky move and hardly the case. It sounds too easy."

"Would you or anyone you know have done it?"

"No." As he answers, his eyebrows shoot up.

"Exactly. Alexius knows how you think. He doesn't know shit about me." Releasing his shirt, I stand up on my feet, slapping dust from my pants. "Unless Roberti has spilled his guts—and he is not one to share what he knows —they don't know what I'll do. I'll see you tomorrow."

"Where are you going now?"

"To get some sleep." I feel his eyes on me until I disappear through the trap door. My mind is spinning with worry and excitement.

Finally, a lead.

Chapter Two

Zoltan stands stock still, fists clenched, and a muscle jumping angrily on his chiseled jaw. Alex and Cassius flank him on either side, both holding daggers dripping with black poison under his chin. His entire body is vibrating in rage, but he doesn't move. When I see Cassius's daughter standing right behind them with a hand pressed on Alex's back, everything becomes clear. All the fighting has stopped, and everyone is staring at the entrance of the portal. A hunter thrusts his blade at my chest, but I spin, grabbing his arm and wrenching it out of his socket. The hunter screams a bloodcurdling sound when his arm dangles in my hand. I drop it at my feet, my eyes never leaving Zoltan's.

"I knew you had it in you, Franky." I recoil from Andrius's voice a second before he steps through the portal.

Dark energy comes off him in waves, darkness dancing like a living cloak around his shoulders. Moving closer to where they hold Zoltan, his gaze traces my body slowly up and down, lingering on the exposed glimpse of my breasts. Bile rises in the back of my throat.

Another hunter inches closer from my side. My arm shoots out, my fingers gripping his throat and my nails digging into his windpipe. My hand curls, sinking into flesh, blood drenching it to my wrist. I open my fingers, releasing the blob in my hand to follow the crumbling body of the gurgling hunter to the ground.

"She is magnificent." Andrius claps his hands in glee, his eyes glittering with madness. "Isn't she?"

"It's me you want, Roberti." Taking a step closer, I ignore Zoltan's glare. "Let him go."

"Why should I do that?" He sounds like we are discussing the price of potatoes at the market. Anger bubbles in my chest. "When I can have you both?"

"You'll have a lot of dead hunters and might even lose your useless life if you don't let him go." Sliding my feet on the floor, I inch closer. "If you think I'll come willingly after you hurt him, you are crazier than I thought."

"I won't hurt him." Andrius, in his right mind, slaps Zoltan's face good-naturedly. My chest vibrates from the vampire's growl. "He is leverage."

"Why are you doing this?" I think I see Leo's tail slinking on the side, but I can't be sure. I slide closer. "What is it you want?"

"It's not what I want, Drake." His face twists in anger. "It's what everyone wants. Don't you see?" Spreading his arm around, he points at the people around us. "Who decided that vampires are the top of the food chain, that the rest of us should crawl at their feet? You think the shifters and the demons don't loathe being guards. Being treated like the dirt under their shoe. Well"—He grins with no humor —"let's see them now. There is a bigger power in town."

"That's it? You are doing this for your ego, you stupid fuck?" I see a hunter creeping closer from the corner of my eye, but I'm too angry to care. "You are killing innocents in Sienna, and in the academy, so you can feel important. You really are a moron, you know that right?"

"You'll see things my way soon enough, Drake," Andrius snarls.

"Now get your ass through the portal, or it'll go down. Alex was smart enough to get enough of your blood to bring all the portals down. Let's see how you feel knowing it's you that is responsible for so many deaths."

"You will not pin this on me." But his words stab me in the chest. What the shifter said to me in the dining room rings in my ears. *"It's all her fault."*

"Don't listen to him." Fenrir materializes next to me, his power holding by a thin thread that's ready to explode and knock us all over. *"He is full of shit."*

"Should I kill him now, and we fight?" Andrius leans forward in anticipation. *"What do you say, Fenrir? With Zoltan dead, you can have her all to yourself."* He leers at me, making my skin crawl.

"He won't kill him," a woman's voice hisses to my right and I stiffen when I catch a glimpse of white clothing. *"He's bluffing, don't be stupid. Let him take him; you can get him out."* It sounds so familiar it takes a moment to place it.

"What the fuck?" hissing under my breath, I'm grateful Andrius is focused on the Fae at the moment. *"Myst?"*

"I got you, chica. That asshat manipulated me, as well. I knew Alex was up to something." She inches closer, raising all the red flags in my head. Fenrir says something I don't hear.

"And I should trust you, why?" Everything is so messed up right now I want to scream until my throat is raw.

"You shouldn't." She snickers like a nutcase. *"But the enemy of my enemy is my friend. He won't kill the hunk. But he can bring the portals down."*

"Fuck me." I breathe and she snorts.

"You're hot and all, but I don't swing that way." When Fenrir fidgets next to me, I know he can hear us and that my time is up.

"What will it be, Drake?" Andrius glows in glee. *"The Daywalker or Sienna?"*

"Zoltan!"

The scream is ripped from my chest when I bolt straight up in bed, drenched in cold sweat. Tears stream down my cheeks, soaking my hair and pillow. Every night is the same thing. Every time I close my eyes, I relive that horrible scene over and over with the same result.

They always take him away.

The door is nearly ripped off the hinges, banging loudly off the opposite wall before swinging back and almost hitting Fenrir in the face. He lifts his arm, palm slapping it away as he rushes to my side. I want to laugh, but breathing is such a struggle at the moment that I can't. My heart hammers in my ribcage with a vengeance. The Fae whirls around, knees bending as if he expects to find someone attacking me. He's been patrolling every night, but I think this is the first time he has witnessed my nightmares.

"I'm fine, Fenrir. No one is there." Gasping the words out, I pull the sheet up to my neck. The white tank top I'm wearing is see through from the wet patches all over it. The last thing I need is to flash my nipples at the Fae.

Fenrir turns around slowly and straightens. His gaze searches my face and a line forms between his arched eyebrows. Not wanting him to see how unsettled the dreams make me, I glance around the room, my eyes landing on random things just so I don't look at him. My fingers hurt from how hard I'm squeezing the sheets at my chest.

"I didn't know you were having nightmares." With a sigh, he lowers to the edge of the bed, the mattress dipping under his weight while his eyes remain glued on me. "I should've known."

"You're not my mother, Fae, nor am I a child. We all relive our failures when you do what we do." I hate that I sound defensive, and I hate even more that he has a sad look plastered on his face. "I don't need you to feel sorry for me, Fenrir. Or responsible, for that matter." Offering him a smile I don't feel, I try to take the sting away from my words. "I'm a big girl. I can handle a few nightmares."

"You know you can trust me, right?" He tugs on my hand a few times before I allow him to take it in his. His thumb rubs soothing circles over the back of it, and I feel my shoulders lower slightly. They were up to my ears from tension.

A harsh snort through my nose is his answer.

"I'm not your enemy, Hellion …"

"Neither are you a friend."

"I know you've been left on your own your entire life but that doesn't have to be the case anymore." He watches me intently, ignoring my previous comment. "You don't have to talk to me about it, but you let Astara in. She is your friend so talk to her."

"About what? That because of me her brother might be dead already? I'm sure that conversation will go well." Yanking my hand back, I curl my knees and wear my arms around them. "I don't need therapy, Fenrir, or to talk things through. That's what humans do. We go kill the fuckers that won't let us sleep." When he keeps staring at me and says nothing, I sigh, deflating. "What?"

"I was going to talk to you about it tomorrow at break-fast"—Swinging his legs up, he gets comfortable by stretching out on my bed, his feet crossing at the ankles next to my hips—"but since we both can't sleep let's make the most of it."

My face twists in a grimace to show him how ecstatic I am about his idea, but I wiggle sideways to give him more room. One cheek jumping in a barely contained smile, he slides closer and leans on one elbow, making himself at home. I have a feeling this is going to be a long night.

"Well? Out with it and maybe I'll get an hour of sleep before everyone starts making noise around here."

"Let me see your finger." Lifting his palm up, his fingers wiggle in expectation for me to do what he asked.

"It healed, I wasn't stabbed in the kidney. Just a stupid splinter." But I do place my fingers in his, letting him turn the said finger this way and that to inspect it. "See? I'll live, unfortunately."

"Hmmm." Shaking his head, his platinum strands slide over his shoulders like silk as he offers me a grim look. "I'm not sure anyone can survive this, Drake. It was, after all, a vicious splinter bred to kill."

I try.

I try with everything in me not to laugh but after a few snorts, bursts of laughter have me clutching my stomach from the serious expression on his face. The corners of his lips twitch a few times too before he joins me, chuckling as well.

"You are such a goof, Fae." Gasping for air, I straighten as a few more giggles pass my lips. "Now that we settled my impending doom named death by a splinter, can I hear what you want to talk about?"

Leaning back, he runs his fingers through his hair, pushing it back over his shoulders. I can see he is thinking how to phrase whatever it is he wants to say. I've been more hotheaded than usual lately because fear for Zoltan's life, for the portals, and everything else is making my head spin. I don't blame him for walking on eggshells around me. I would slap some sense into my own head if I was in his shoes.

Good thing he knows better than to try.

"I've been observing you ever since I saw you in the bar in Sienna." Referring to the night when I visited my friend Daren's bar in hopes to get drunk and drown my sorrows, Fenrir brings back memories I'd rather forget.

I was suspended from the Special Forces for the Accord where I worked as an agent under Roberti. Fenrir apparently was there to check out who he would be dealing with in person. I brushed him off, storming out of the bar and spending a good amount of time that night riding my bike through Sienna aimlessly to clear my head. It was the night I was assigned to infiltrate the academy. It was also when everything went to shit.

"It's nice to have time to sit back and observe while the rest of us are fighting for our lives." I flinch at my comment because I said it out of spite and to shake off the feelings that came with thinking about how naïve I was. "I didn't mean that."

"I know you didn't." Scratching his jaw, he eyes me contemplatively. "That just supports my observations actually. You see we know now that Roberti was playing the long game, especially with you. While we were too busy with distractions, which I have no doubt he orchestrated, he was placing all the chess pieces on the board. Lucky for us, and very unfortunate for him, he underestimated you just like everyone else."

"I have no idea what that means," I tell him honestly, pointing a finger at his face. "I will never be a pawn as long as I breathe."

"No, you were never meant as a pawn." I almost thank him, but he ruins it with his next words. "In his game of chess, you are meant as the queen." A grin spreads across his face at my scowl. "What he didn't expect was for the queen to start kicking like the knight, tracking him like the bishop, and blasting him like the rook."

"I don't play chess, Fenrir. I'm too busy surviving. Get to your point."

"That's exactly it, Drake." His hand flicks at me as he speaks, all the muscles in his arm jumping under his skin and distracting me for a second. The Fae needs to be less attractive if he wants anyone to actually pay attention to what he is saying. By the knowing grin he shoots me, he is aware of my exact thoughts in this moment, too. The jerk.

"Roberti thought by giving you his protection he would mold you into an obedient soldier for his cause. He never expected your trust issues to be so rooted that what you showed him would only be a small facet of who and what you really were. A mask, albeit a real part of Francesca Drake. His arrogance will be his downfall."

"And what? You think you know the real Francesca?" A sharp ping of fear spears through me but I don't show it, instead keeping my face impassive. "I don't even know who or what I am."

"Far from it, but I'm slowly learning. Before you try to bite my head off, let me finish." I press my lips closed hard because I almost tell him what I think about his learning. "As I said, I think that played well for us to even tweak his plans as much as we have so far. But it's not enough and I think you'll do much better—we will all do much better if we train you properly on how to use your powers. You do astoundingly well by acting on instinct and impulse. I must say I'm impressed, but you lack discipline. I'm worried that it'll cost you in the long run."

"I …" His eyes turn into slits when I open my mouth, knowing before I do that I am going to talk shit just for the sake of pissing him off. My mouth closes with an audible click, my nostrils flaring.

"I'm not going to say you're not right in your *observation* because we both know you excel in your stalker tendencies. Stop smiling, though. It's creepy as fuck." No amount of glaring can wipe the smirk off his pretty face. "Anyway, we don't have time to train or whatever else you have in mind, Fenrir. Thanks to that asshole Alex, they have a lot of my blood to mess with the portals, plus they have Zoltan. We can't sit behind these walls playing training camp. Not now."

"True." Giving me a very royal-like incline of his head, I can see the wheels turning behind his eyes. "That's why I have an offer for you, Hellion. One I think you will like." He rushes to assure me when I fill my lungs to speak.

"What kind of an offer, Fenrir? If I know anything about the Fae, that's to never make a deal with one. You'll always get screwed at the end." After I realize what word I just used, I stab a finger at his nose. "Don't even go there. There will be no screwing with anyone."

"Such a prude." But he laughs, proving he loves pissing me off as much as I love doing it to him. "I will not cage you inside these walls. That was never my intention. But instead of aimlessly searching for leads and sneaking around, we can use that time to strengthen your powers while looking for Zoltan. I will train you myself. Leo offered as well."

We look at each other with our gazes locked for a long time. On one hand, I know he is right. All this time I've been winging it, using whatever comes to me on its own to survive the situations I am thrown in. On the other, urgency is stabbing like the claws of a beast in my chest to get to Zoltan because time is running out. My head is spinning with indecision, and I want to say "let's do it" at the same time as I tell him "no way am I training now." Fenrir startles my by jumping off the bed and striding to the door before I can realize what he is doing.

"We start right after breakfast. Sleep well." Throwing it over his shoulder, he closes the door before I can protest, leaving me with my mouth open and a million curses I don't get to say.

Chapter Three

"You are not even trying, Drake!" Fenrir barks at me for the fifth time.

He is lucky I don't have the power to shoot daggers from my eyes, otherwise he would be in trouble. Grinding my teeth, I hold my tongue, not because I don't want to tell him where to stick his attitude, but because the damn shifter is prowling circles around me looking for an opening while the Fae is distracting me.

"Leash your dog, and then let's see how tough you are Fenrir," Leo snarls, saliva dripping from his long canines at my jab.

"Less talking. You haven't even chipped the illusion." Ignoring both of us, Fenrir paces in front of me with his hands folded behind him on his lower back.

Trees stretch high all around us. The clearing where the three of us stand has a shimmering portal to the right, winking in and out of existence just enough to keep pulling my attention to it. Moonlight streams through the treetops, so at least I'm not fighting blind. It catches on Fenrir's platinum hair and Leo's fur from time to time giving away their position. Occasional snarls and hoots of owls and other birds add to the mystery of the night where predators roam in search of their next meal. Predators like the three of us.

No, we are not outside in the woods surrounding the academy. We are in one of the training halls inside the building where the Fae can unleash his power unchecked. Even the scent of uprooted soil and wet grass mixing with the stench of decaying plant life is so real I have to force myself not to look impressed. He really doesn't need anything to increase the size of his arrogance.

"I might like keeping you here in the dark, Fae. Better to toy with both of you this way." I'm hoping he can't see me wiping the sweat out of my eyes or squinting like an idiot in hopes to see through the thick shadows.

"You are too focused on things you can't do rather than the things you can," Fenrir lectures, undeterred by my bullshit.

The air stirs at my back and I twist around just in time to see the large wolf sailing high at me. Adrenaline punches my stomach like the hooves of a horse, my breath getting stuck in my throat at the razor-sharp jaws coming for my neck. My instincts take over, and spinning around on bent knees, I tuck my shoulder under the massive beast. Flinging him over my head, his body smacks one of the tree trunks on the opposite side of us. My entire being vibrates in sync with the thundering of my heart.

"Like going for and grabbing everything you can physically touch instead of what you can mentally break." The Fae is insufferable. "Leo just proved my point."

"Leo might need a minute to lick his balls now that I

cracked him in half." Gasping for air, I grin when the shifter growls menacingly from the shadows. "Aww, it's okay buddy, all dogs think they are wolves until they meet an alpha."

The shifter comes out of nowhere, ramming me from the side. All air leaves my lungs in a hard whoosh when I hit the ground, the back of my head slamming with a hollow thump. If I was human, my skull would have splattered like a melon. Dark spots take over most of my vision, my mind spinning so fast bile rises at the back of my throat. The monstrosity I hide inside me wakes up, poking its head out for the first time. I can feel how eager it is to come out and show what it can do. As usual, I clench my teeth and push it down while holding Leo's jaw open with both hands, stretching it as wide is it can go without breaking it in the process. The shifter keeps snarling, drooling all over my face and neck.

I guess the comment pissed him off.

"You are holding back, and that is a weakness too." Fenrir lives in his own world, his voice coming from somewhere above my head to the left. "You are here to push your limits, Drake. Not to play it safe. You continue to force control when you don't need it."

"You have no idea what you are asking for Fae." Pushing the words through my teeth, I buck my hips hoping to get the over-two-hundred-pound beast off me. He is crushing my ribs. "If I don't control it, I'll bring the building down on our heads. Is that what you want?" His words are muffled from the hair-raising growl coming out of Leo. I think the shifter is trying to make me pass out with his dog breath. "What?" I have no idea why I'm asking the Fae to repeat himself.

"The walls of this hall are fortified to withstand magic.

Stop restraining your power and break the illusion. The sooner you do that the sooner we can continue with something else. You are wasting time."

Anger bubbles like lava though my veins. They are the ones wasting time by staying here instead of being in the human world looking for Zoltan. Now he is blaming me for his ridiculous ideas. The shifter rakes his claws down my arms, opening gashes. The pain fuels the anger, weakening my resolve to have control of something none of us understand. Letting lose when hunters are trying to kill us is one thing. Doing it around innocents is another, and definitely not something I want to do.

"Stop hiding behind the mask, Drake. Let Francesca out —the real Francesca Drake. Not this poor excuse of a timid half-blood you're giving me."

Calmness washes over me when the rage his words provokes reaches a boiling point. Warmth spreads through my limbs, taking the pressure from the shifter on my body away. Leo is still on top of me but I can barely feel the weight. Colors swirl and come to life around me, the night blooming before my eyes as bright as a day. Blinking slowly, I zone in on the wolf's face and the widening of his intelligent eyes vibrates my chest with a satisfied purr. Leo's hackles rise, and with a yelp he jumps off me, wrenching his jaw out of my hands.

I flip on my hands and feet, one knee bent to my hips before my face lifts to look at the Fae. Magic pulses through me and stretches my skin tight. Fear flashes in Fenrir's gaze for just a second before he gives me a smirk to cover it up. I know my eyes have changed and resemble a dragon's with a vertical pupil. It's only when they change that I can see everything has its own heartbeat around me.

"It's time you take off your mask as well, òg rìoghail," my voice purrs, husky and foreign to my ears.

Fenrir takes a step back, the blood draining from his face.

"There you are, fuil dràgon." Shaking off whatever spooks him, the Fae bows low, his ponytail brushing the ground at his feet. I have no idea why that makes me happy or have a newfound respect for Fenrir. "Francesca needs your help to understand you are not separate from her, that the two of you are one and the same. She is young and in need of guidance."

"You want me to roam free." Lifting to my feet, my eyes narrow on the Fae. Black and red colors twist around him like a living thing, reaching out toward me before shrinking back as if afraid. "To what end? What is it you want?"

"I have sworn to guard the dragon blood. That is my only purpose." Fenrir barely finishes his sentence before I attack him.

Pushing off the balls of my feet, my body collides with his, sending us tumbling into the trees. Not just the sound and the scent. Even the feel of his illusion is real, rattling my bones when we hit the thick, gnarled roots. The pulsing of power in my chest explodes outward like a blast of scorching-hot air dispersing it. Pinning him under me and making him gasp from the pressure of my knees on the side of his chest, I see Leo slinking around from the corner of my eye. The walls and open space of the training hall is revealed, too bright in the light of the floating flames placed strategically on the walls after the darkness the Fae waves around us. Moonlight brightens the windows creating patterns on the mat-covered floor.

The glamour Fenrir keeps close to his skin like a cloak breaks apart too. The blue of his eyes is replaced by all black with a pupil as white as snow at the center of it. His cheekbones sharpen so much I will cut my finger if I trace them, and his lips take on the color of fresh blood. Pointed ears twitch under my gaze and his platinum hair is now a waterfall of midnight black fanning around his head like a pool of oil. Parting his lips in shock, he blinks a few times, his long, thick lashes casting shadows under his eyes.

"There you are." I grin at him. "Now we are on even ground."

Leaning my face close to his, I can feel his breath puffing over my skin. My braid falls on top of his hair, the blonde color of mine contrasting with his dark strands like the first ray of the sun piercing the night. I struggle to get control of my power, to push it back where it can't hurt him. As much as he pisses me off, I don't want to do any damage to the Fae. And from the feeling I get inside me right now, I know my power wants to play with him like a cat with a mouse. I'm going to strangle Soren for not teaching me how to leash this monster.

"Enemies have discovered your bloodline." Fenrir is much braver than I give him credit for. His Adam's apple bobs up and down, but his voice is calm and even. "You need to be whole to survive what's coming. I cannot protect you on my own."

"You think I need protecting. Perhaps the worlds need to be saved from me." Tilting my head to the side, I stare into his eyes. If not for struggling to push this creature back and be myself again, I may have found them freaky as hell. "What of the Daywalker? You think him weak?"

"They are waking the old gods. Zoltan and I are not enough." Lifting his chin, Fenrir impresses the crap out of me when he manages to look down his nose at me while I'm pinning him like a bug. "Apart from Soren, who is untouchable unless they destroy themselves along with him, you are the last dragon blood alive. If you don't merge fully with her, you'll either perish or end up imprisoned and used as a blood bank. The choice is yours. I will still die to protect Francesca till my last breath." Both our heads snap to the right when a shadow falls over us. "Leo, no!"

Fenrir's roar does not stop the shifter from attacking. The green color of his eyes is nowhere to be seen, and in its place is an amber gaze like a tiger's eyes glittering in the orange light when he pounces on me, his jaws snapping an inch from my jugular. Still keeping the Fae immobile between my thighs, my arm shoots up, the heel of my palm connecting with Leo's chest with a sickening crunch. The large wolf sails over us and hits the mats on his side, a pained whimper falling from him and stabbing me in the heart.

"I will not be used," I purr at Fenrir, turning away from Leo like I don't care if he is still alive. I scream inside my head, scratching mentally at the monster controlling me right now. "Have your wish, òg rìoghail, but remember one thing as well as you remember your true name. The power of dragons was given to this bloodline when we retreated from the worlds. It can easily be taken away, leaving you to destroy yourselves like you are so determined to do. Do not play games with me. An seann fhear might be entertained with them. I don't possess his patience."

"Mo 'fhacal agam, fuil dràgon." I feel power binding Fenrir to me when he speaks.

Pain like never before bows my back. I scream to the skies, the windows of the hall bursting from the sound into millions of pieces. Glass showers over and around us like pouring rain, the sound muffled by the roaring in my ears. My bones are melting, all my insides are shredded and mushed into a pulp. It feels like I'm being skinned alive, the muscles of my body cramped and contouring. It lasts for eternity, and every second I wish it will just kill me and be done with it. When it's over, I'm left in a boneless heap twitching on top of Fenrir, panting for breath. I'm no more than a whimpering mess.

"What ... did ... you ... do ... Fenrir?" Every word hurts as it comes out from my raw throat.

"What had to be done." I wince when he wraps his arms around me and kisses the top of my head. "Just breathe. The pain will be gone in a second."

"What did ... I call you?" I have to swallow twice to finish that sentence.

"Young royal"—The incredulity in his voice is loud and clear— "in Gaelic. And before you ask, I called you dragon blood."

"You said something else, too. I felt the words binding you, you idiot." The pain is almost gone, so I thump him weakly on his chest.

"I gave my word to protect you. It's a binding I freely offered." When I try to look at him, he grabs the back of my head to keep me down. "Rest for a moment longer; you'll feel sick if you stand up."

"I think I hurt Leo badly." I don't fight him because I'm not sure I won't empty my stomach all over him if I do stand up. "There was something wrong with him."

"He will be fine. He's healing as we speak. Leo is an alpha, so his animal reacted to your power. He attacked on instinct alone. I don't think Leo had any control over it, just like you didn't." His fingers massage the back of my skull, relaxing me further. "And just so we get it out of the way, I do not regret binding myself with the oath, Drake. That was not acting on instinct or for self-preservation. Maybe now you can trust me a little." I can hear the smile in his words even if I can't see it on his face.

"I'll try," I mumble, my head shaking along with his chest when he chuckles. "I'll still kick your ass if you piss me off."

"I wouldn't dare think otherwise, Hellion."

Chapter Four

"How is he?"

After leaving Fenrir to take care of Leo and following the Fae's orders to take a shower and eat something again, I descend the winding stairs leading under the academy. Since I haven't been down here before, it takes me quite a few wrong turns and opening doors to empty rooms to find the infirmary. They must've seen quite a bit of fighting before I got here to have a place full of all sorts of medical equipment. All of us heal fast but after having the experience with that poison the hunters are using that turns everyone feral, I see the reasoning behind it. One of the medics, a mage, snarls at me to keep my hands to myself when I try to push some buttons on a machine. Crestfallen, I hurry to find Leo's room before I get in real trouble. Curiosity and medical equipment do not go together.

"He is not dead yet and can speak for himself," Leo grumbles like an old lady, and Fenrir grins when I roll my eyes.

"I thought you'd be catching up on your beauty sleep,

princess." Plopping on the chair next to where the shifter is sitting on the bed, I shove my hands under my thighs to resist the urge to press buttons. "I'm sorry for what happened, Leo." He might get on my nerves, but I had no intention of hurting him that badly. I make sure he sees that on my face.

"That was all my fault." His animal jumps to the surface, looking at me through his eyes. "I haven't lost control like that since I first became an alpha. I should've expected you to test me."

"What's that supposed to mean? It's not like I did it on purpose." Guilt is eating me alive and making my stomach lurch. I definitely sound defensive. "If I want to kick your ass, I'll do it like this. Not while my powers are out of control with a mind of their own."

Glancing around, I search for a bucket or something. I shouldn't have listened to Fenrir when he forced me to eat. Right now, all the food is about to come back out. My nails dig in the padding of the chair while I flare my nostrils, breathing in and out slowly. Leo gives me a cocky grin, the green color of his eyes slowly returning. Fenrir, being Fenrir and all, watches me in disapproval with arms folded over his chest.

"We can give it a go, Drake. Any time." The shifter winks, unperturbed by my scowl. "What I meant was, I should've expected the reaction of my wolf when your dragon took control." My mouth opens and closes, gaping like a carp out of water. "Nothing can prepare you for that until you experience it. Holy shit, that was something." Chuckling, he shakes his head.

My eyes snap to Fenrir and the jerk has the decency to look abashed. I can see all the bullshit that is about to come out of his mouth and it fuels my anger even more. Before he speaks, I shove a hand at his face, which makes him snap his mouth shut and press his lips in a thin white line. I can't believe this shit.

"You actually planned that?" My words are soft and barely above a whisper. If I talk louder, I may scream until they hear me all the way across the portal. Leo winces, his shoulders jumping to his ears when he realizes his slip up.

"Now, listen Drake—" he starts but I don't want to hear it.

"Let me get this straight, *friend*." Lifting from my slouch, I square my shoulders. "Your idea of getting me to trust you was manipulating me to train where you'll force me to release the control I have over my powers. The powers that none of us know anything about, may I remind you."

"It was the—"

"And you thought it was a great idea." Talking over Fenrir, I glare at Leo. He at least looks like he feels bad. A few broken ribs and a punctured lung can do that to a person, I suppose. "So, you were like, hell yeah let's do that. She'll spill all her secrets and we'll be bff's, huh?"

"May I speak, Drake?" Fenrir grinds the words through his teeth.

"No, you may not," I snap at him.

Leo snorts, covering it up with a cough.

"I could've killed him. That's how much I cared what happened to either of you at that moment. I will not have you manipulate me to satisfy your Fae fetish fantasies of me calling you a royal, bowing and speaking Gaelic."

This time Leo chokes, almost coughing out a lung. I hope it's the healthy one so he gets stuck with the one I punctured. Fenrir's cheek jumps, and for his sake I hope its anger causing it and not him fighting a smile.

"He wasn't playing games." Leo coughs, tapping his chest to stop hacking.

"Of course he wasn't. I'm a pigeon according to him." Huffing in frustration, I jerkily fold my arms over my chest so I don't strangle them.

"I never called you that." The Fae is looking at me like I've lost my marbles. Leo's head is spinning from me to Fenrir like this is a tennis match.

"Yes, you did. You said I'm a chess piece that kicks around and blows shit up. A pigeon, punting all the pieces off and shitting on the game board." Leaning forward, I dare him to deny it.

"This is something from human television." Pressing the bridge of his nose with a thumb and a forefinger, Fenrir squeezes his eyes shut and I almost think he's in pain.

The shifter roars in laughter and my ears ring from the volume of it. It's absolutely unbelievable how they can't see how wrong everything they do is. And they call me impulsive and unreasonable. Not even I can beat that level of stupid if I try. I'm about to tell them that when the door of the infirmary room bangs open, bouncing off the opposite wall.

A mage with her red hair twisted in a tight bun on the back of her head marches inside with a stern look on her pretty face. Not even the freckles sprinkled over her cheeks and nose soften the fire burning in her green eyes. The symbol from the front doors of the infirmary—a drop of blood circled with sigils—gleams gold on her right upper arm. She heads right for me and I jump out of the chair I am occupying.

"All three of you can leave right now." Hissing at me, she snatches my arm and drags me out the door before I realize what she is doing. "I have patients here still trying to recover after the attack on the portal. You are disturbing their peace."

She shoves me out the double doors and I stare at her with my jaw hitting my chest. I'm too stunned to speak. She disappears for a moment, returning with Fenrir whom she also practically throws through the doors. The Fae stumbles, catching himself at the last moment before his face hits the wall of the hallway.

"Hey! I was hurt and recovering," Leo protests, his voice getting louder the closer he gets. He is shoved through the doors too, barefoot and wearing only the bottom part of pajamas. His top is thrown at his face next, tangling around his head.

"If you can laugh and make noise then you don't need to be recovering." Glaring at all of us, she slams both doors in our face.

"What just happened?" An incredulous chuckle comes from me while I'm still watching the doors wide-eyed.

"You met medic Aspen." Yanking the pajama top off his face, Leo snarls at the closed doors. "Her bedside manner leaves things to be desired."

"If you don't leave in two seconds, you'll be in need of recovery when I throw a curse at you." The voice of medic Aspen is clear as a whistle, and I wonder if she's waiting behind the doors because she knows the shifter will talk shit about her.

Still laughing because I don't know how else to process this, I grab the males by the arms and tow them down the hall with me. Fenrir looks insulted and Leo is dragging his feet, still twisting his head to glare at the door. I bet he wishes he had x-ray vision. I tell him as much.

"Wouldn't that be convenient. If only the fates were so kind," he says wistfully, making me laugh for real.

"I think I like medic Aspen." Chortling at the horror on their faces, I keep shoving them in front of me.

It takes me a while to push them toward the office room we've been using as our base of operation ever since Zoltan pulled me and Astara out of Argoz's class. The whole way the training hall incident keeps replaying in my head over and over. By the time I jerk them inside and close the door, all my anger and frustration is gone and I'm left tired to my bones. A lump squeezes my throat when I think about Zoltan and how he should be here with us but I swallow it down. Even the papers are still spread over the long table, which is exactly how he left them.

"I think I'm going to give it a try," I tell them both as I drop on one of the chairs closest to the window.

They both look at me like they don't remember I'm here. Leo is sitting gingerly at the edge of his chair holding his upper body straight. I'm guessing his ribs are still smarting. Fenrir, on the other hand, is draped like a throw rug over his, one of his legs swinging over the armrest, his eyes closed, and his face turned up like he is sunbathing like the humans I watch on TV from time to time. He turns his head and blinks at me when I speak. I'm glad his glamour is back in place. It unnerves me to look at his white on black eyes.

"To trust you." Obviously, I wasn't clear enough. "Neither of you can be that good at lying or manipulating, not when you are stupid enough to almost get yourselves killed while trying to rile me up so I lose control. But none of that matters because I'm giving you a chance. If you blow it, that's all on you." Shrugging one shoulder, I look down at the papers on the desk so I don't have to look at them.

It might be stupid after everything that happened with Roberti and my entire life in general, but no matter how I spin the situation, I know I can't do it alone. If not for me, I know they'll do what's right for Zoltan. It's the only thing I've got right now. Easier said than done but I'm willing to try.

"You have proven that you are loyal, Drake." My gaze jumps to Leo's face when the words rumble from his chest. Grinding his teeth, he stabs his arms through the holes of the pajama top. "My animal won't hesitate to fight by your side, and neither will my human side. That's not something you can force or buy with empty promises. I like to make jabs to piss you off, but that's the shifter's way when we like someone. You've earned my respect, which means I'll always have your back."

Not knowing what to say and doing everything I can to stop the tears burning the back of my throat from falling, I give him a stiff nod. Emotions are trying to choke me but I manage to push them down. The warmth that spreads through me from hearing that and the content pulse of my power startles me enough to snap me out of it before I make a fool out of myself. Fenrir hasn't said a word yet, just keeps watching me like I'm a bug under his microscope.

"I make no promises, but as I said, I'm willing to try." I shrug again, more of a nervous twitch than a conscious movement.

"You will not regret it, Francesca." When he does speak, Fenrir sends a tremor down my spine with how serious his face is.

"That's to be seen, Fae." Shaking off the shivers, I roll my neck to release the tension building at the back of my skull. "What do we do now that you have awakened a beast?"

"The beast was awake, just a little lazy." Fenrir accepts

36

my change of subject by winking at me. "Now we see what the moles will be stealing from the library."

"Come again?" All the stiffness is gone from Leo, the predator in him perking up at the idea of a hunt.

"Drake here was exercising the strength of her upper body by climbing the walls from the outside last night." The Fae chuckles when I narrow my eyes at him. "It was quite entertaining I must say." Turning to Leo, he grins.

"You really are a jerk, you know that?"

"Trusting me does not make me less of a jerk, Drake." Fenrir is so serious that Leo is turning red in the face so he doesn't laugh. "It only makes me a trusted jerk." Bowing at the waist—which is an amazing thing to do while being draped over a chair—he jerks back. "At your service."

Leo loses it then. Not even cracked ribs stop him from laughing his ass off at my expense while slapping his thighs again and again. I rub a hand over my face and lean back in the chair.

"This is going to be a disaster," I tell them both with a sigh, the words muffled from my hand.

Chapter Five

True to his word, Fenrir doesn't tell Astara or Argoz about the demons stealing a book from the library. That's the reason why I'm hugging the top of a bookshelf, breathing dust and inhaling spiderwebs. As soon as we get Zoltan back I'm going to petition the Board to assign maintenance here for fuck's sake. The roof is cleaner than the library.

And they call themselves an academy. Lazy fuckers.

Someone opens the large doors, footsteps smacking an even rhythm over the wooden floors. Holding my breath, I peek with one eye from above their head to see who walks in. I've been rolling in nasty up here for over an hour while the place shows no sign of life. Cemeteries see more action than this library. A female with a cloud of thick chocolate curls strides purposely between the rows of bookshelves. Her muscular build and swaying round hips mark her as a shifter. Anticipating something like this, Fenrir placed an illusion over me to hide my scent. She would've known I'm the resident rodent the moment she opened the door without it. Releasing the breath I'm holding, I pull back and press my cheek on my folded arms. If the demons don't show up soon, I'll fall asleep. Thanks to the nightmares, I'm lucky to even get an hour of shut eye each night.

The shifter doesn't linger long, finding what she is looking for within minutes. Then she leaves and closes us in. Leo and Fenrir are somewhere in this humongous place, destroying their lungs with dust too. We spread out so we can have a visual no matter where that important book is placed. It's a good thing the wide, wooden bookshelves are lined up so close together. It makes jumping from one to the next a lot easier. I just hope they are as sturdy and unmovable as they look. With my track record of causing trouble without trying, I won't be surprised if they start falling like dominos the second I move.

My mind keeps going back to the night Zoltan was taken. It's not like I had great dreams before, but I keep thinking the reason I'm seeing it night after night is because I'm missing something important. A headache with its own heartbeat develops at my temples. Filtering the air by using my shirt and breathing into my elbow, I try to center myself, to push the fear for his life and the hatred for Roberti aside. Watching it replay in my mind's eye by simply observing it makes me wonder why I haven't done this before, but sitting here in the deathly silent library is as perfect as any place.

Detaching from the situation, I watch the hunters—the white color of their clothing easily recognizable—spread around methodically, which is to be expected since Alex and Cassius will know how the academy will react to the threat. They strategically separate the shifters and Fae from the vampires, hoarding the mages between them while leaving the demons mixed in with all of them. A lot of demons don't make it out alive, so I can't lump them all as traitors. And then there is Myst, weaving through the chaos while dressed as a hunter. I can't figure out the female no matter how hard I try.

The fight was going well for us until they got their hands on Zoltan. But how? If it was anyone else I would say they blindsided him. But almost as if he has eyes in the back of his head, nothing gets past the Daywalker. So they must've tricked him, which tells me I was unwillingly used for it. It's the only explanation that makes sense, and everyone has pointed out how irrational he has been acting since the day I stormed through their gates. Roberti's words float in my head about everyone being sick and tired of feeling inferior to the vampires. Seeing their attitude in Argoz's class, I can kind of see his point, but that's the only time I've seen it. Could it be he has been telling the truth and we have passive moles who secretly support his insanity because they really are tired of feeling like a second fiddle. It's a ridiculous thought but crazier things have happened. It may carry some weight, so I'll store it away to think about later.

The door cracks open, jerking me out of my musings. This is the wrong time and place to reflect on things, but I feel like I'm onto something. First: catch the thief. Second: solve the puzzle. Very slowly, I tilt my body sideways, peeking down from my perch. My heart jumps in my throat and lodges there when I see a demon squeezing his broad shoulders through the crack in the door. He could've opened it wider, but I guess he is as invested in his role of sneaking around as I am in mine to lurk and catch him righthanded. I have no idea what time it is or how long we've been waiting, but judging by the protesting of my arms and legs, it's the middle of the day in the human world. A time when most people in the academy are sleeping.

Glancing over his shoulder, his hair tangles around one

of his curling horns before he slides inside. Holding the door so it doesn't move, he waits for the second demon to slide in, this one taller but also thinner—even though he still looks massive in comparison to say … me. Smirking at each other, they push the door back without closing it. Huh. Maybe it makes noise and they are trying to be subtle. They'll know more than I do in any case. With barely any noise and while walking mostly on the balls of their feet, they each head a different direction, probably to see if anyone else is here. The fact that they don't even look up is stupid of them. A few moments later, they meet at the open space near the doors, both of them shaking their heads as if telling each other no one else is in the library.

"You checked everywhere?" the first demon to walk in asks, his voice recognizable from the night before.

"No one else is here." The second voice confirms that these are the two Fenrir and I heard from the roof.

"Let's grab it and leave before someone decides they need a night read." The first one is already walking between two wide rows of bookshelves. I'm stretched out on the fourth one to their left, watching them like a hawk.

"I'm sure there will be wards or some type of protection around it," the second one mumbles, his head turning left and right. I have no doubt he can feel that he is being watched. His buddy can too if he stops acting tough and being a dick.

"That's why we have this." The first demon pulls something from his pocket, waving his closed fist through the air in front of his friend. "It'll break any protection they've placed around it. Now quit stalling and move. The sooner we grab it the sooner we'll be out of here."

They pass under me while he is talking, so I flip around and wait for them to get ahead before jumping on top of the next row of shelves. A shadow moves to my right and I see Leo crab crawling like a pro on his side, moving closer to the demons to follow them. Still no sign from Fenrir but I can feel him close by.

"I have a very bad feeling about this," the second demon—and I decide he is the smart one out of the two—says as he cranes his neck to stare over his shoulder. "Maybe we can come back tomorrow."

"You are a coward and a disgrace to all demon kind," the first one spits in anger. "I have no idea how I got saddled with the likes of you."

"Wanting to keep my head attached to my neck is not being a coward." The smart demon hisses, but his shoulders hunch up when his buddy is not watching. I make a mental note to be sure to tell Fenrir this guy will be easy to crack and that he will sing like a canary.

As silent as the wind, I move from one row to the next. Leo keeps pace on his other side, throwing glances my way from time to time. Watching him from the corner of my eye, I pick up his trick of stretching between bookshelves before moving to the next. It's faster than jumping for sure. Clever shifter.

When they reach the end of the library the demons turn right, walking under Leo's nose. I grind my teeth when I realize I'll have to jump a lot further to get to that side. The shifter watches me unblinking and nods in encouragement. I don't need courage; I need the damn shelves to be closer. Without debating it too long, I jump so we don't lose the demons. There is a split second where I freak out, where I think I push too hard and am about to raise the dead from the amount of noise I'm about to make, but somehow, I land in a crouch an inch from the edge of the shelf.

Leo grins at me, his teeth flashing white in the low light.

With a tight smile, I follow his lead and crawl behind him. Unlike any shifter I've ever known, Leo, an alpha, gives me his back to show exactly how trusting he is of me. My hands are shaking from the adrenaline coursing through my veins. I'm not used to people getting enjoyment from working with me. My ex-partner Aiden is a prime example, his bad attitude and suspicions are what I'm used to dealing with. Until now, that is. My smile grows. Maybe it's not stupid that I'm giving the whole trusting them thing a shot. I like this team work much, much better.

Leo stops moving and crouches as low as he can, staring intently at the demons. Shuffling closer, my thigh brushes his when I squeeze next to him and peer over the edge. The two traitors are facing a simple wooden door, one I don't even know exists until this moment. Glancing at Leo, I can tell it isn't a surprise to him, but I can also see he's so pissed that if a snake bites him right now the thing will die of poisoning.

"You keep watch. I'll grab it," the first demon tells the other, lifting his fist where he is clutching the thing from his pocket.

A crystal the size of my thumbnail twinkles innocently when he catches it between his fingers. Not stepping closer to the door, he stretches his arm and runs circles with it in the air. Sparks burst when the crystal connects with the protection wards, an impressive display of sigils lighting up and coming to life. They flash bright red one second then fizzle out in the next. The twinkling crystal in the demon's hand crumbles to dust on the floor. I'm too stunned to do anything but watch him disappear through the door, popping out twenty seconds later with a thick leather-bound book under his arm. My blood curdles in my veins when the title stamped in gold catches my eyes.

Barathrum Tartarus.

I may not be very well versed in Latin but even I recognize the book that all the supernatural world thinks is destroyed. The Abyss of the Underworld was burned when they imprisoned the Titans, ensuring they could never be summoned again. And here it is, as safe as a babe cradled in the demon's arms. When I turn my face to Leo, a sharp ping passes from my back through my chest. He doesn't look surprised at all to see it.

Now that the demons have what they came for, they move as fast as arrows back to the library's doors. I push my unease aside for later, following the demons behind the shifter. Anger comes off of him in waves. Mine matches his but its mixed with betrayal. We watch the demons bolt through the door before dropping down on the floor. I only have time to bend my knees in hopes to soften the impact before I'm flying after Leo.

The hallway is empty when we exit the doors and panic numbs my skull that they are lost to us. At the end of it and to our left, Fenrir pops out of nowhere to wave us along. I guess he isn't in the library anymore, which is a good thing since we may have lost the demons otherwise.

Reaching the end of the hallway, we only catch a glimpse of Fenrir's back before he disappears around another corner. Through twists and turns and down secret stairways we descend, that is until we exit the academy from the door at the side of the building, which is a well-used hidden entrance if I've ever seen one. I don't have time to think about how many traitors have used it to kill us off one by one, though. Not yet.

In silence, we round the path circling the building, catching a glimpse of Fenrir entering the wooded area on the opposite side of the main entrance to the academy.

Jumping over gnarled roots and fallen trees, we finally catch up with him. The Fae finally stops our sprinting by raising his arm. Hidden in the shadows of the trees are the two demons, and they are standing at a portal I don't know about until this moment.

A third figure bolts out of the trees so close to us I'm surprised he doesn't see us, or hasn't seen us before now. Hunched up and constantly looking over his shoulder, I expect guards to be right on his heels. Leo has made sure the shifters are busy with other things tonight, however, that way they won't spook our thieves. Whoever this guy is, he must just be paranoid. When the light from the swirling colors of the portal reveals his face, Leo grabs my arm to hold me back.

"I know that weasel," I hiss under my breath. "He was attached to Cassius's daughter with a belly cord."

"Leave him for later," Fenrir's body coils up, his power punching me in the face and buckling my knees. My fight or flight instincts flare up at the sound of his voice. "Get the book by any means necessary."

In the next breath, Leo shifts and the Fae launches at the demons.

Chapter Six

I stand back for a second and watch the two demons. They are so focused on the guy running for them they have no clue death has written their names at the top of his list. Fenrir might want the book safe more than anything else in this moment, but my feet are glued to the forest floor, my entire being centered on the guy I recognize. Recalling the conversation from the demons, I remember them saying the book will be given to Alex, and by default to Andrius.

That's the guy I want.

A harsh wind blasts me like a punch to the face when Fenrir's power sends the two demons flying back, their bodies flipping head over heels until they hit the trees behind them. The demons don't stay down long, jumping to their feet and doubling in size. I zero in on the book, which has been flung to the side. The force from the power the Fae unleashes snaps it open, making pages flutter before they finally settle. My chest vibrates from the impact of the wolf colliding with one of the demons, their bodies smacking hard when they meet high in the air. Leo's wolf is magnificent stretched out in flight, and then his body curls around the demon, his claws sinking in and tearing flesh.

Fenrir is not so lucky. His demon is more focused on getting away from the Fae, so he runs through the trees and disappears in the forest. His high-pitched scream tells me he didn't get too far before the Fae is on him. In the few seconds it takes for everything to happen, my eyes land on the dark-haired guy, who is as frozen in place as I am. The air shimmers and flickers in tune with Fenrir's target, warning me I have less than one second to get my hands on the guy. My whole body tenses in preparation to pounce on the guy, but he wakes from his shock as well. On instinct, my right shoulder turns to the side because I expect him to bolt the same way he came in. To my surprise, he sprints right for the book, his beefy arms pumping while he is pushing through the dense air drenched in magic.

The monstrosity inside me perks up, but unlike before it stays just below the surface of my skin, there but not really there. It's unnerving, like two people occupying the same body. All that bowing and sprouting bullshit in Gaelic might have been useful. Points to the Fae if I can find a semblance of control. My feet tingle through my boots where the magic feeding the academy answers, almost as if Soren is giving me his approval to do what I need to. I can never be sure with the old fart, though. He is too lost in his own world and too unpredictable to be able to count on.

The tips of my boots barely touch the ground as I hone in on my target, running diagonally across the clearing to intercept him before he reaches the book. My vision wavers from one blink to the next, and his life energy bursts out, muting every color around him. My thighs are flexing with each step closer and I almost sway to the side when I feel my pupils expanding and contracting to bring him more into focus. That will take some getting used to.

The beefy guy's head turns in my direction and all the blood drains from his face. The vein on his neck jumps hard once before it starts pounding so fast the idiot might have a heart attack. I have no clue what I look like ,but based on the pale-corpse impression he's doing, I bet it's not a pretty sight. Snarls and roars mix with flesh hitting flesh around us. I have to give it to the guy. He doesn't turn to run from me. A second more passes, his eyes flicking from me to the book and back again as if he's trying to decide if grabbing it is more important than staying alive.

His jaw clenches with determination and he puts a new burst of speed behind his movements, forcing me to turn at a sharp angle to even have a chance of stopping him before he reaches the book. From the corner of my eye, Leo swipes his claws at the demon he is fighting, his muzzle opening and snapping only inches from the demon's neck. Dark patches mat his fur in places, which tells me he must've taken a few hits himself. The air shimmers and twists again and I grind my teeth. Fenrir better not screw up with his illusion. If I lose the guy, I'm going to kill him myself. The demon fighting the Fae must be keeping him busy if he hasn't done it yet, though. That works just fine for me.

Another blast of power slams into my chest coming from the trees where Fenrir is fighting. It flings me back and I land on my ass. My tailbone screams in protest, my teeth jarring when I land. An audible "*oomph*" escapes me as I scrape the shit out of my palms when I try to soften the impact. Jumping to my feet, I see beefy guy lifting on his knees and shaking his head. They could've picked a smaller clearing and I would've had him by the throat a long time ago. Nothing is easy for me in this damn place. Scrambling up and kicking rocks and dirt behind him, he runs again. I bolt too, almost parallel with him now, but still not within arm's reach.

We stop at the same time, the open book between us.

"Oh hey." I grin at him, more a baring of teeth than a smile. "Nice to see you again. Remember me?"

It looks like his eyes are about to pop out of his head, his face still as white as a sheet of paper. Red capillaries spread like lightning strikes through the whites of his eyes. Chest rising and falling fast—and it has nothing to do with the running—he stands frozen like a deer in headlights. His gaze flicks to the book between us and back to my face again.

Not so scared after all.

"Take it." My body is so tense I'll tear a muscle if I move. He startles at my words and my grin grows. "I dare ya."

Leo yelps and my heart jumps to the back of my throat but I don't dare look away from the guy. We are now in a standstill, both of us waiting to see who will move first. I'm not worried that he will grab the book and get away because this is more of a game now. I feel the purr vibrating my chest, the excitement of toying with my prey before I kill it pumping through me. Tall trees burst from the ground, making me flinch back in surprise. The trunks stretch up around me, the dark gray bark on the trees seeping thick sludge that emits a cloying, sweet scent. Gnarled branches spread out, thick and twisted like the large knuckled fingers of a skeleton reaching for the sky. There is no leaf in sight. In no time at all, the illusion settles, and beefy guy is hidden from me. I curse up a storm in my head.

That's what you get for being cocky, Franky.

"Seriously, Fenrir." Shouting my anger, I try hard to

recall where the damn book was before he messed everything up. "You couldn't fucking wait a second?"

The jerk laughs.

His voice floats through the trees like he is everywhere at once. Damn Fae and their games, even in situations like this. I should expect him to get so caught up in the fight he pushes everything else aside. On the bright side, beefy guy won't know where it is either. I just need to find him, then I'll grab the book when the illusion disappears. At least I know how real Fenrir's illusions are. Definitely not going to touch anything.

I pick my way through this forest of death and shadows, choosing carefully where I place my feet so I don't make a sound. Twigs and what looks like old, yellowed bones litter the floor.

"You can break the illusion." A breeze ruffling the short hairs around my face carries a whisper.

Right.

Nails biting the skin of my palms, I breathe through my nose. The sweet scent fills my lungs like poison choking me. For a second, I wonder if Fenrir makes this shit up, pulling it out of his tight, too perfect ass, or if he can only create what he has already seen. Goosebumps cover my arms with the thought that where I'm standing now is actually a real place somewhere. There is no moon in the sky or stars. Light gray fog like cotton presses the tips if the trees, silver lightning flashing through it. Everything is void of color, leaving nothing more than a monochrome world stretching as far as my eyes can see.

Crack!

The snap of a twig or a bone coming from somewhere in front of me is as loud as a bomb going off, echoing through the trees. If what I recall in my mind is right, beefy guy is moving closer to the book. Stopping my movement, I close my eyes and concentrate, pulling on the power thrumming through me just enough to hopefully activate that strange vision where life is revealed. I'm not sure if I break the illusion if he is too close to snatch the damn thing.

The beast inside me answers my call eagerly. The burning under my skin is uncomfortable but somewhat bearable. When I open my eyes, my stomach clenches from all the shadows pulsing and reaching from the trees. The muted red glow from between two large trunks identifies beefy guy, but I stand staring at all the darkness around me. My brain is trying to recall the memory of the terror from seeing the swirling shadows in Sienna devouring a soul. Cold sweat trickles down my back and numbs me.

The guy moves again, and I stay still to give him the false hope that I don't hear the sound he makes. The red glow that pulses from him gets brighter, slinking closer to where I'm still glued to the spot. It's enough to help me push down the memories that will make me curl up in a ball. Wiping my damp palms on my pants, I finally make my feet move again. The guy is closer than before but still not too close if my calculations are right.

When I can clearly see the outline of his life energy, I yank on my power as hard as I can. It's like a blast ripping through my ribcage, my heart stuttering like the wings of a butterfly before my ears pop and the illusion around me blinks out. *Surprise, surprise, Francesca Drake miscalculated.* Beefy guy is standing right on top of the book, the open pages spread out between his feet. This time he doesn't hesitate. Not even offering me the time of the day, he bends down, grabs it, and runs. That brings my stupid brain back online.

I bolt after him.

"No you fucking don't." Snarling at my stupidity, I pump my arms to gain on him.

The guy is fast. I never check to see what he is, but someone as thick as he is should not be running like that. My mouth dries out when I see that he is not trying to go for the forest to lose me or hide. Oh no, that will be too much to ask. The idiot is shooting like an arrow right at the blinking portal. What are the odds that he will miss the timing and be unable to get through? Judging from my previous experiences and luck, I say I trip and faceplant on the ground before he screws his timing up.

Something comes to life at the corner of my eye, moving fast and closer to us from the tree line separating the academy walls from the clearing. I'd love to see exactly what or who it is, but beefy guy is nearing the portal and I don't have the luxury of satisfying my curiosity. If it's someone trying to help this asshole, I'll deal with him after I get the guy. I push with everything in me, my fangs dropping and throbbing in my mouth.

The guy, book gripped in one hand with pages flipping hard enough to rip, reaches the portal just as I'm close enough to grab him. My hand snatches his shirt, my fingers twisting in the fabric. I yank on it as hard as I can, my upper body bending to reverse the momentum. The sound of tearing fabric splits the air, much too loud to my ears. His outraged roar of denial follows soon after. His arms, one hand still holding the book in a death grip, windmills in hopes to shake me off, and I hear Fenrir's shout behind me.

"Drake no!" the Fae roars, but whoever is moving towards us has reached us.

Beefy guy pulls forward hard, jerking me enough I think my arm is going to pop out of the socket because I have no intention of letting him go. The front part of his body

52

enters the blinking portal. The other person reaches us, slamming full force into both of us. I lock eyes with them for a second. Stunned by a familiar blue gaze, my mouth drops open.

"I got him," Astara snarls, grabbing the guy and realizing her mistake a moment too late. Gravity snags us in its clutches.

All three of us hit the portal hard, and my whole world turns upside down.

Chapter Seven

I hate fucking portals.

My insides feel like they are being ripped apart then rearranged so I can fit through the tiny hole in a piece straw. It hurts so much that my brain flips a switch, turning off so I don't scream. It'll be useless anyway. No one can hear me in this nothingness of swirling colors where I want to die and puke at the same time. Squeezing my eyes shut, I can't even summon enough energy to freak out when Astara is ripped away from me. At least my hand is so cramped it's stuck in the position of grabbing the asshole who got me in this mess in the first place, so I can't let go of him even if I want. Which I don't. My braid swings wildly, slapping me across the face and arms. Now I also know what it feels like being whipped with a rope.

I should chop the damn thing off.

It lasts forever, this unending tearing of my insides. Being prevented from screaming only makes it worse. I taste blood in my mouth, probably from biting my tongue. The coppery flavor flows down my tight throat. Bile hits the roof of my mouth, while tears rain down my face from my tightly shut eyes. *At least I still have the fucker*, I keep chanting in my head. I'm going to kill him very slowly the moment we are out of here.

I'm spit out none too gently on the other side, the stench and noise of the human world overwhelming my senses. The weight from the jerk disappears from my outstretched arm, and I drop on my knees vomiting even the food I was fed as an infant. Cold sweat drips from my face like someone has poured a bucket of cold water over my head. My entire body is shaking so hard I'm practically lifting off my knees with each new wave of bile. When the white noise in my ears quiets, I almost laugh hysterically when I hear the asshole is not having any less fun. This time is worse than my first for some reason. When I open my blurry eyes I see why.

Colors pulse and dance around me, only adding to my dizziness. Since I was pulling on the magic inside me when I broke the illusion in our realm, I never actually released it. Sitting back on my haunches, I wipe my mouth with the back of my trembling hand, squeezing my eyes shut with a pained groan when a bright beam blinds me. It's like a dagger being stabbed in my brain. I pitch to the side, catching myself on one arm when something bumps into my shoulder. Squinting, I watch Astara stumble forward and grab the guy by his hair, yanking his head back.

"You motherfucker, where is my brother?" Her pretty face is twisted in a mask of rage, her snarl showcasing her fangs in all their glory.

"Get the book." I gasp for air and try to lift myself up.

My elbow gives from my weight and I drop back on my ass like a freaking turtle that's unable to flip over. There is not enough strength left in me to push back the stupid magic, let along to stop the swirling colors stabbing me behind the eyes. Plopping on my back, I give up the fight and just breathe through my nose, while the guy sounds like he is giving birth. Panting and gagging, he has yet to answer the question.

"Don't let him get away." My lips are moving but I'm not sure any sound is coming out.

"He is not going anywhere." Dread crawls up my throat at the sound of her voice. *I guess I did speak.*

"The book." Blowing air through pursed lips, I remind her why we are here.

"I thought you were looking for a way to find my brother when you were creeping around." The accusation is loud, clear, and like a punch to my chest. "But this was more important?"

Something hits me on the side of my thigh. Still not daring to open my eyes, I fumble weakly with my hand and search for it blindly. The tips of my fingers brush against the pages of the book. I guess she's so pissed off she kicked it at me. Scratching at the leather, nails digging to get a purchase, I pull it close enough to have it under my arm. My chest caves from the deep sigh that passes my lips.

"I never stopped looking for him." Mumbling the words, I manage to lift my other hand so I can rub at my eyes. "That asshole will lead us to him. We just can't let him take the book to Roberti."

Astara is quiet, but I finally stop feeling like I'm about to die. *It's the little things Franky,* I tell myself, wanting to laugh at how stupid that sounds. Slowly, my body feeling like it's been through a tenderizer, I sit up, feeling empty now that I manage to push the magic away. Blinking away the residual moisture from the tears, Astara and the guy come into focus. My friend is still holding him away from her feet by the hair, probably so he doesn't puke on her boots. She gives me an accessing once over when our eyes meet.

"You look like shit." Her lips twitch.

I look down at myself and have to agree with her. Dressed all in black, my clothing is covered in dust and spiderwebs from crawling all over the library shelves. Cold sweat has the fabric sticking to my body, creating even darker patches in spots. Hair has escaped my braid and is sticking to my neck and face, while my thighs and sleeves are sprayed with vomit. I don't even want to think what my face has on it.

"I look like the end of days survivor." I sound more awed than disgusted.

Astara snorts.

"What is that damn book anyway?" Instead of answering her, I flip it over so she can see the golden writing on it. "Fuck!" Her hand releases the guy when she takes a step back.

"Yeah." The guy topples over on his side and I roll my neck, eyeing him. "Sounds about right. So I want to know where he was going to take it."

He groans.

"How did he get that?" The way she snaps the question tells me she's not surprised that the book is not burnt like it should have been.

"Any other important details the rest of you are hiding from me or does this top the list?" Pushing off the ground and taking the book with me, I make sure I don't look at her. I can't right now. "What other fresh kind of hell is hiding in that academy that I should know about since, you know, my life is tied to it and all?"

"Franky, I didn't hide anything from you." She takes a

step closer but my raised arm stops her. "That thing was under wards and I haven't thought about it for decades."

"That's kinda stupid don't you think?" Locking gazes with her, I grind my teeth. "I'd think that would be the first thing to pop in your head when we have unidentified shadows devouring people through Sienna. And when your brother has been taken by a demigod who's threatening us with the biggest power we've ever seen." I dare her to say anything to defend herself.

"I thought he was talking about using you to achieve it." Her eyes flick to the book and I'm shocked to see the fear there. "No one could be that stupid. Not even greed for power could make anyone do something suicidal like using that book."

I look around for the first time. Another alley, this one void of dumpsters, stretches on both sides. Gray walls tower over us too, smooth and windowless. My stomach drops to my feet when, ahead of us, I see the reason the light stabbed me in the brain when everything was bursting with color earlier. There is some sort of roof stretching between the buildings, leaving this part dark and shadowed, but not where the entrance of the alley meets my eyes.

Daylight.

I start hyperventilating, and not even knowing that it can't reach me here can stop the panic raging inside me. I've never seen daylight. Oh I've seen it plenty on TV, but not like this. Not with my own eyes. Something hard hits my back and I realize I am pressing myself to the building and clutching the book to my chest like a shield. Frantically, my eyes dart around so I can assure myself those rays will not come from anywhere else. Yes, I am half Fae, but I'm also some weird, unknown origin that may or may not be able to handle sun well. I'm also half vampire, and although my blood apparently makes Daywalkers, I still might turn into a charred corpse if I step foot in it.

"Francesca, calm down." Astara's voice breaks through the buzzing in my ears and I lock my gaze on hers to ground myself. "It's okay. It always feels like that the first time you see it. Breathe."

I can't speak so I give her a few jerky nods so she knows I hear her. Everything I believed my whole life so far tells me to shrink back and make myself as small as possible so the death rays don't reach me. Facing a hundred hunters in close quarters is better than this. Hunters I can fight. I have a chance of survival if it's a physical enemy. I can't fight the sun. Other than the moon pushing it to sink below the horizon, nothing can. A rational part of my brain is telling me I might be overreacting a little, but the terror is drowning it.

A bright burst of light makes me shriek, plastering me to the wall so much I'm almost molded to it. It's lucky I'm rooted to my spot of darkness or else I might do something stupid, like bolt into the death rays. The fact that the mouth of the alley is far enough for me to be safe does not even register right now. Fenrir pops out of nowhere with Leo in his wolf form right next to him, close enough for me to feel the bristling hairs of the shifter on my legs. The Fae jerks, his gaze searching the alley. When he finds me, his outstretched arms freeze, but he looks like he's ready to tackle me.

"If you make me move from this spot, I'll rip your throat out before the death rays kill me." My voice is a little more high-pitched than I'm comfortable with. I'll have time to feel mortified for acting like an idiot when I stop freaking out, and not until then. "I'll take you with me."

"The sun." Astara flings a hand and points at the mouth of the alley when Fenrir turns a confused face her way.

I swear the damn wolf is laughing at me.

My leg jerks on its own and I kick him harder than I want. He snaps his death trap of a jaw at my knee, but not even that can force me out of my spot. The asshole that caused all this scrambles to his feet, probably thinking we are too busy to stop him. Well, *I'm* too busy freaking out, but Leo isn't. He pounces on his back, slamming him face down. It's quite satisfying to hear the crack of his forehead and the breaking of his cartilage against the concrete. My body relaxes and my heart slows, even though it is still galloping against my ribs like a racehorse.

I thrust the book at Fenrir.

"You got it." His shoulders visibly relax the moment his long fingers wrap around it.

"No thanks to your idiocy with that illusion." Remembering I'm pissed at him, I snatch the book back. "I thought we were supposed to be getting the book. Isn't that what you said oh mighty Fae?"

Yup, the wolf is snickering. Creepy.

"I got a little carried away." He has the decency to look crestfallen. "They did not fight like typical demons." He frowns at the unconscious guy with an over two-hundred-pound wolf sitting on his back. "They were faster … stronger."

"Typical of a male to underestimate his opponent," Astara hums in agreement. "Can we go back now?"

My brain is still clouded with fear but the panic is at a somewhat bearable level. That helps for me to actually see Fenrir instead of just his face. His hair has escaped the elastic band leaving it wild around his shoulders and chest. His tight black shirt is shredded to shit where the demon has raked his claws. Blood makes the tattered fabric stick to his defined muscles, which are visible through the tears. The leg is also ripped on his right thigh, the pocket of the tactical pants hanging sideways like a gaping mouth. Leave it to Fenrir to still look ready for the cover of a magazine even with the smudge of dirt across his left cheek and forehead. I can just see the headline: "Wild and Sexy."

My brain is definitely messed up.

"You okay?" Astara touches my arm and I'm proud that I don't flinch.

Little things Franky, little things.

"No, but I'm better." Turning away from Fenrir's intent gaze, I blow out a breath. "I didn't mean to freak out like that, sorry," I add lamely. "It's just … I didn't expect it, and I don't know why."

"If it makes you feel better, I actually clawed my way up my brother's back the first time I saw it." Astara snickers. I crack a smile imagining how Zoltan reacted to that. "It's a hard instinct to fight. You are doing better than many males I've seen."

"That doesn't say much." Even Fenrir chuckles at that. "Can we go back now?" I repeat my question, my fingers rubbing over the leather book.

"We need to get to a portal to go back." Fenrir sighs. I can tell the Fae is itching to get his hands on the book I'm holding.

"We can wait for night to come here, right?" I sound hopeful, handing it over just so they don't notice my hands are shaking while holding the heavy book.

"Or we can try and go now." At the horror on my face, Fenrir rushes to make his point. "You don't know if you can walk the daylight. All I'm saying is we can try. We will retreat if you can't and wait here."

The bustling of the world across the mouth of the alley is like a siren song. The idea of actually being there, seeing it all bathed in the golden death rays is more appealing than it should be if I had an ounce of brain functioning the way it should. Astara's comforting squeeze on my arm pulls my gaze to her. She is as nervous as I am. Even Leo stops panting, his tongue hanging to one side in excitement. I push off the wall, squaring my shoulders before I lose my shit and curl up on the nasty ground. Keeping my eyes locked on the light, I stride toward it as dread rakes its claws through me and fear almost chokes me. Clenching my fists, I don't even slow down when I feel the warmth of it wash over my skin. Astara and Fenrir hover right at my back. Everything in me screams to turn back. An insane idea pops in my head.

And when have you ever done something smart.

Closing my eyes, I step out of the shadows.

Chapter Eight

My heart stops right before it starts thundering so hard and loud it mutes the honking horns and sounds of life in the city. The sting on my skin is uncomfortable but not painful, so I stand still even though I'm ready to bolt back at the first sign that something is wrong. A smile spreads slowly, growing so wide my cheeks hurt from it. That's until I open my eyes.

With a high-pitched scream, I jump back and cover my face. The fires of hell are blazing behind my lids and melting my eyeballs. Astara pulls my face to her chest and squeezes me tight, saying something to Fenrir over my head. They sound like they are arguing but it's all just noise because of the agony I'm in. I can't catch a damn break in this cursed life of mine. Is one day with no pain too much to ask? Is one thing going right for me too much to hope for?

Tears stream down my face and soak my friends shirt, her chest vibrating against the forehead I'm pressing on it. Her fingers move up and down my back, soothing and calming as they ride the excruciating pain with me. The heat from Fenrir's body disappears from my back, telling me he has moved away. The hum from their voices is gone too. I have no idea how long Astara keeps rubbing my back and rocking me gently in her arms, which is something my own mother has never done. The sound slowly returns, my brain scrambled from first the portal and now this.

"Shhh," Astara coos. "I'm sorry, I didn't think it would be that hard on your eyes."

"This one is on me, not you," I tell her shirt, still afraid to open my eyes. "You suggested, but I could've said no."

"Good thing it's an easy thing to fix." She pulls back to hold me at arm's length. I squint at her, eyes open like slits.

"How? Buy new eyeballs?" Sounding dejected, I rub my still-watering eyes.

"I have something better than that," Fenrir pipes in, entering the alley. I didn't even know he left it.

"I don't want anything from you." Blinking fast, I finally see more than just blurry outlines and distorted faces. "Every time you offer something, shit hits the fan and I'm the screwed party."

"She figured you out, Fenrir." Astara giggles, her voice tinkling like chiming bells.

"I'm not doing anything to purposely hurt you." He shoves something black at me and I swat it away.

"I'm not doing anything to purposely piss you off, yet here we are." When he looks at me deadpan, I grin. "Not all the time anyway."

"Put them on." He shoves that thing in my hands again.

Sunglasses.

I almost laugh.

Turning them in my hands, I watch the black, round plastic, flicking the handles open. The lenses are big enough to reach from my forehead to halfway down my cheeks. Lifting them in front of my face, I point them at the Fae.

"I'll look like a fly wearing these." He purses his lips. "Did you get some clothing too? If you didn't notice, I'm a mess. I'll scare the shit out of any human we come across."

"I'll use illusion so no one will see us." He waves a hand at himself, pointing out that his clothing is ripped as well. Yet he walked among them to get the sunglasses.

Stabbing the sunglasses over my ears, I lift my face and stretch my arms in front of me. Waving them around, I slap Fenrir's chest and face while pretending I'm blind. Astara laughs when he grabs my wrists and scowls at me.

"Oh, I didn't see you there, Fenrir," I tell him innocently, my voice pitched like a child. " Great job of hiding the death rays from my peepers."

""I'll carry the male." Releasing my wrists, he strides to where Leo is still perched on top of the asshole. "We need to go. Maybe we can even question him before going back."

All my humor disappears with those words. When the agony melting my eyes stops, I feel so relieved I almost dance from happiness. Reminding me of why I'm even here is like someone dousing me with a truck load of reality. The pressure returns to my chest and prevents me from fully expanding my lungs.

Fenrir returns carrying the guy in a fireman carry over his shoulders. Leo trots next to him, his ears pointed up and one flicking at every noise that sounds. They pass us, disappearing in the daylight without a word from the Fae. Astara folds her arm under mine and takes me with her.

My second attempt at facing the death rays is much better than the first. I'm still too chickenshit to fully open my eyes so I'm squinting through the glasses like an idiot. At least my eyeballs are not melting, which I consider a win. It doesn't take long for my curiosity to make me forget everything apart from this new world. In another life, I must've been a feline shifter. There is no other explanation. I would use my brain to be more careful otherwise.

Humans dressed in warm clothing duck their heads in the collars of their jackets while rushing wherever they need to go. Cars streak by moving in both directions, the drivers honking or yelling out the open windows. Doors open and close from stores and businesses, letting out music or chatter that floats through the air with each exit or entrance. Laughter dances around my ears, and I find myself smiling while rubbernecking so I can see it all. Night was beautiful and familiar the first time I was here. Day is something totally different.

"They act differently during the day," I tell Astara while she guides me by the arm, waving pedestrians through so we don't bump into them.

"They feel safer in the daytime." She looks around too, as if trying to see what I see. "I haven't paid them much attention."

"Why?" My forehead scrunches up in confusion. I find them fascinating.

"We deal with hunters mostly when we come across the portal." Sighing, she hurries after Fenrir, who is walking like he owns this world. "Or some other problem needs fixing."

"Like what?" My eyebrows lift when I notice the Fae swinging his arm with the book in his hand. "He should've hidden the book instead of waving it around."

"He is casting an illusion so no one can see it." I still feel uneasy even with Astara's assurance.

"Where is the portal?" I can't help but ask when we turn a corner and a stretch of residential buildings stretches in front of us.

"I guess Fenrir wants to question the traitor before taking him back to the academy." I stiffen when Astara takes a meaningful breath. "I know you've been avoiding me because you think I blame you for what happened, Franky."

"I am to blame," I rasp out, guilt thickly etched into my tone. "They wanted me. They took Zoltan instead." A lump forms like a fist in my throat.

Fenrir and Leo enter a building on our side of the street through glass double doors. I bite the inside of my mouth, not knowing what else to say to break the oppressive silence between us.

Swallowing thickly, I clear my throat. "I'll get him back alive if it's the last thing I do." I promise her, and it's the truth. I won't stop until he is back where he belongs, even if that means I trade places with him, portals be damned.

"We will get him back. And stop blaming yourself and avoiding me. Roberti and Alex are to blame, not you. As well as Cassius and that bitch of a daughter of his."

I hum just so I don't have to tell her she is wrong. We move up the couple of stairs to the double doors and enter the building as well. A decorative rug sits in a circle at our feet. Two small side tables with large vases full of plastic flowers hug the wall on either side of us. Two elevators, their stainless steel doors showing us our reflections, are in front of us across the decent-sized lobby. No low-cost apartments for the Daywalkers, that's for sure.

Astara stabs the up button placed between the two elevators and I stare at the red-glowing numbers above the one to our left. My thoughts return, the same ones I had while stretched out on top of a bookshelf in the library. Roberti's words are like a haunting song replaying in my mind. The elevator dings, the door slides open, and we both step inside, Astara pressing the top button. Leaning on the metal bar, I press the side of my head on the mirrored wall and breathe through the freefall feeling my stomach gets when the metal box jerks and moves up.

"It's not what I want, Drake. It's what everyone wants. Don't you see? Who decided that vampires are the top of the food chain, that the rest of us should crawl at their feet? You think the shifters and the demons don't loathe being guards. Being treated like the dirt under their shoe."

Roberti's voice is so loud in my head it's like he is standing next to me screaming the words in my ear. Closing my eyes, I snort air through my flaring nostrils, barely holding myself up from the weight pressing on my chest. Now that the adrenaline is gone from, seeing beefy guy trying to get a book to Alex—with help from the demons from the library of course—has a whole different meaning. How many of the others feel the same as the three we upper handed? Andrius is insane and power hungry for sure, but how much of what he said is true? The elevator jerks to a stop and I numbly follow Astara to the only door on this floor.

Fenrir left it open for us, so we walk into a huge open-plan apartment. The living room and kitchen are separated only by a long slash of a marble counter. Three leather couches, warm chocolate brown, are facing each other in front of a cinema-sized flat-screen TV. A coffee table that looks like an old-time suitcase is placed between them, decorative books set messily on top of it. Marble tiles cover the floors, the sunlight coming through the wall of floor-to-ceiling windows reflecting. The city stretches in front of me, and it's beautiful. A long dining table is right in front of the windows, chairs surrounding it. One of those chairs has been pulled to the center of the empty space and beefy guy has been dumped in it.

Fenrir throws a glass jar full of water in his face just as we enter.

"Wakey, wakey, princess." Leo walks in from a hall to our left, tugging a pair of sweatpants up his hips. Beefy guy gasps, coughs, and flails in the chair.

"Let's start with where Alexius is." Casually, Fenrir walks up the marble slab and places the now-empty jar on it with a soft clink. "Then we will move on to your great idea about stealing from the academy." Turning around, he leans his back on it and folds his arms over his chest.

Hair plastered around his head, water and blood mixing and dripping from his face, beefy guy jerks his head to look at each of us in turn, his eyes so wide there is more white than anything else in them. "You are going to kill me anyway, so why should I tell you anything?"

"True," Leo grins at him wolfishly while scratching at his chest. "It's up to you if you die fast or very, very slowly." If it's possible, the guy pales even more. "What's it going to be princess?"

"Why did you do it?" Everyone in the room looks at me when I speak but I ignore them and focus on the guy, staring at him through the stupid sunglasses.

"I have nothing to say to you half blood," he snarls at me, spittle flying from his mouth.

Leo clocks him in the jaw so hard his head snaps back and he topples on the floor with the chair. Grabbing him by the hair, the shifter yanks him up, straightening the chair before dumping him in it again. Dusting his hands by slapping them together, he waits for a second to see if the guy will fall again, but the asshole just looks dazed.

"Now answer her question," Leo says cheerfully. A shiver passes through me. I know he is an alpha, but I never imagine he will be like this while beating someone up.

"I don't know." The words are thick, like he bit his tongue when Leo punched him.

It goes as expected. Every question we ask, the answer is always the same. He keeps saying he doesn't know. I have to step in twice before the shifter kills him, too scared we won't find anything about where to look for Zoltan, or if he is dead. The whole time Fenrir leans on that damn marble slab, his face impassive. He doesn't say a word. That's until his entire body stiffens and his head jerks to the front door that we left open.

"Oh look." Myst leans on the door dressed all in black leather, her blonde hair streaked with white highlights, the hilt of a sword sticking up from her back. "It's a party and I wasn't invited." She pouts at Fenrir who looks ready to faint or run.

How interesting.

Chapter Nine

"So," Myst drawls, pushing off the door and striding inside the apartment. "What are we doing?" Her head tilts this way and that as she checks the half-conscious demon on the chair. "Cool look on you, Chicca. It's a definite deterrent for males." She swirls a finger at my face and person as she passes by me.

"I was on a mission," I mumbled while subconsciously swiping my fingers over my chest, as if that will make me look less like an apocalypse survivor.

Astara snickers and Leo grins.

"Oh no, babe. You have it down to an art. The blood-sucker will dig it, I promise." She walks a slow circle around the chair before giving me a very serious look. "He will know that no one peed on his territory while he was away on business. They love that shit. Trust me."

I stare at her for a long moment half expecting her to laugh. Even a smile would do the trick at this point, but she is watching me with such a straight expression that I turn to check the others in case I'm missing something. Astara is testing a new shade of red on her face while doing her best not to burst out laughing. She looks like a puffer fish, her cheeks blown up to hold her breath in. Leo has his lips folded in, biting on them while staring at his feet with his nostrils flaring. Fenrir, on the other hand, has a hand covering his eyes and his face scrunched like he is in pain.

"Am I right?" Myst nods eagerly at Astara. "Males eat that shit up for breakfast. It saves them the caveman act of pounding their chest and growling 'mine' in everyone's face." She stabs a finger at me. "Your hunk is busy being held against his will but that's semantics. You're onto something. Keep at it."

Astara howls with laughter, completely losing it.

"What are you doing here, Myst?" Fenrir snaps, his tone louder than necessary, although it's probably a good thing because otherwise he won't be heard over Astara and Leo laughing their asses off.

"What have you got so far?" Myst comes to face me like the Fae hasn't spoken.

I search her face, still not sure what her game is. She did say I shouldn't trust her, and I don't. She's been working with Alex for fates knows how long. For all I know she is still working with him, gathering intel so they are one step ahead. That's the cynic in me with a mountain of trust issues talking. Myst doesn't look away, her dark brown eyes open and steady on my sunglasses. There is something about her, obnoxious behavior aside, that tells my gut she can be trusted. Just not to what degree. One thing is certain: Myst takes care of Myst first. Everything else is second.

"He was going to meet with Alex." Jerking my chin at beefy, I don't dare mention the book. Fenrir has enough brain to stash it somewhere where it's not visible. "So far, the information we found is '*I don't know*.'" I do my best impersonation of the assholes voice.

"That's it?" Arching an eyebrow, her expression tells me she knows I'm full of shit.

"He was working with two demon guards." Thinking fast, I spin it the best I can without revealing too much. "They were meeting to hash out stealing something from the academy but we chased them to the portal. This one went through with me attached to him."

"Atta girl." Myst winks at me. "Nothing gets away from you. What did they want to steal? That might give us all we need to figure this out."

"We don't know …"

"They wanted to snatch something from the library." Astara speaks over me. I'm not sure if the rest of them notice the slight stiffening of Myst's shoulders. "They didn't get whatever it was."

"Where is Alex, Myst?" Fenrir still has a stick up his ass. It's like he is glued to that marble slab. He hasn't moved an inch from it.

Very slowly, her head turns his way. Since I'm watching her profile so closely, I don't miss the muscle in her jaw twitching when she locks gazes with the Fae, although her features are blank otherwise. Fenrir's face is like a storm cloud ready to unleash a torrent of pouring rains on us. I've never seen him look at anyone with so much disgust. A smirk as sharp as a razor blade blooms on Myst's lips.

"If I knew where he was, I would've brought you his balls as a peace offering, hot stuff. I hear you can make earrings with stuff like that. Some tribal shit for good luck or something."

Waving his glower away with a flick of her wrist, Myst glides around me and pulls the sling of the scabbard over her head. She flings herself on one of the couches, placing the sword gently next to her thigh. Crossing an ankle over one knee, she wraps her fingers around the six-inch needle-sharp heel of her boot. My eyes widen behind the sunglasses she wears. Those boots may be a better weapon than her sword.

"I see I need to make an offering first to be included in the cool kids' club." She swings her foot by rocking the boot she is holding by the heel. "I've been moving around the city, but Alex hasn't shown his face in any of the places he frequents." Locking eyes with Fenrir, her smirk comes back. "That includes his bed, yes."

"What of the hunters?" Leo pipes in. "Any sightings? Any unusual behavior? They can't all just vanish from the face of the earth; it's unlike them."

"On that I have a lead." Myst gives the shifter her attention. I can feel Fenrir bristling. "I came here to actually leave a note about where I'm headed tonight in case I don't make it out. If they get one on me, the rest of you can follow the breadcrumbs."

"Whose place is this?" I murmur to Astara, missing whatever Leo says.

"Zoltan's." Astara gives me a meaningful look, and I have every intention of digging for more details.

"Now that we are done with all the lies, let's get back to the beginning." All conversation stops between Myst and Leo, and everyone turns to me.

Myst grins like I did something monumental.

"Hello Myst, how nice to see you." Jamming my fists on my hips, I glare at her. The sunglasses are killing my death look, but I'm not brave enough to remove them with all the sun coming through the windows. "Why are you here?"

"Leaving a note is a smart move …" Leo trails off, his eyes snapping to Myst and flashing dangerously.

"Leaving a note for Zoltan so he can see it after we rescue him?" The sunglasses slide down my nose so I jerk them back up with my forefinger. "Try again."

"There is still hope for you," Myst tells Fenrir and the shifter before releasing her hold on the heel and leaning forward with forearms on her knees. "I felt the disturbance in the portals and I followed you here. You've been holed up for a while and I figured I should come see what's up." All the attitude melts from her face and she sighs. "I've been monitoring the portals to see who goes in and out. Alexius is nowhere to be found since that night, but I do have a lead that he will be attending a meeting tonight. Your turn."

"We might've screwed up your lead because asshole over here"—I flick a thumb to my right at beefy—"was supposed to meet Alex today to bring him whatever they stole from the library." Myst waits patiently and I take a risk. "They wanted to steal a warded book. We stopped them."

I know I make the right choice because Myst relaxes fully for the first time since she showed up at the door. The lines tugging on her eyes and mouth smooth out and she leans back, sighing as she closes her eyes. I don't know if she knows which book they wanted or not, but when she opens her eyes and looks at me, her movements are less stiff and more natural.

"Nothing is screwed up. Alexius doesn't know you have his worms. The difference is, instead of them we will show up." She cracks her neck, rubbing her shoulder with a wince. "It's all about timing, and where he will be tonight is a perfect place to follow him and spook him out."

"I'm in." Astara is first to agree, her worry for Zoltan as big as mine. "Where are we going?"

"There is a gala tonight organized by the Red Cross to celebrate their accomplishment in opening over ten new hospitals in Africa and South America in the last month. Alexius will be there without a plus one." Myst checks her nails like they are the most fascinating thing in the world.

"He is not going to show up there," Fenrir drawls, arrogance oozing out of him like sap. "Not after how he showed his hand. He had Zoltan at knife point, or did you forget that?"

"What does that have to do with the book?" I frown in confusion, but I doubt they can see it because of the large sunglasses.

"The academy was invited as well." Leo grabs a chair, rolling it backwards before he straddles it and presses his forearms on the back. "Showing up would be too cocky and reckless, even for him."

"The academy supports the Red Cross? That's so nice of them." Maybe Zoltan was right. My crappy experience notwithstanding, the place might not be that bad if I give it a chance. Myst snorts in a derogatory way. "What?"

"Blood, Chicca. It makes the world go round, and round and round ..." She spins her finger at me.

Right. Of course, they'll shove their noses in a place where there's blood. How stupid of me to think those old farts on the Board will do anything that doesn't serve them. I should've talked to Argoz instead of ignoring the ghoul. He would've mentioned it for sure. He was too excited about the party they threw for me when everything went to shit to be able to hide it. More what-ifs and should'ves to add to the pile.

"Fenrir might have a point." Astara grinds her teeth while yanking on her hair in frustration. "He would be too stupid to show up there."

"Who's going?" I turn to the Fae and he looks at me like I'm nuts.

"No one, of course." And there it is, the staring down his nose at me done in perfection. "We have more important things to do than mingle with humans for the sake of appearances."

"What time and how do we get there?" I turn to Myst, ignoring Fenrir's protests.

"It starts at eight pm at the Los Angeles Convention Center." Tapping a finger on her lips, she looks me up and down. "Normally I'd say we should be fashionably late, but in your case that might be a necessity."

"She's not going," Fenrir snaps. "Go mingle with humans. Do what you do. We are going back through the portal where we can find a way to clean up the mess your boss created."

"Fenrir—"

"No, Drake," he cuts me off whirling on me. "It's what she does. Creates chaos wherever she goes with no thought to the collateral damage she leaves behind." Laughing humorously, he shakes his head. "We couldn't get you to do anything else but search for clues on how to get Zoltan back, but somehow she manages to convince you to go to a party in five minutes flat. That's how poisonous she is."

Whoa. Taken aback, I gape at him, my chest feeling tight at the hurt crossing Myst's face. She handles it much better than me. I would've cracked his skull halfway through the nonsense spilling out of his mouth. Not that I know Myst at all, but she is giving us a lead. None of us are here for an evaluation of her character and I don't see anyone else jumping in to offer any help. She is giving us a chance. A chance we can't afford to overlook since until today we have absolutely no idea where to start. Chasing our tails is the only thing we've been capable of for days.

"I'll go get us something to wear." In the deathly silence that follows her words, Astara gives Fenrir a pitiful look and strides out of the apartment without glancing back.

"We can't leave this one here. I can tie him up but I'm not sure it'll hold him long without someone keeping an eye on him." Leo sighs, his eyes anywhere other than on the Fae.

"I have a place where we can stash him until you take him back with you." Lifting off the couch, Myst grabs her sword.

Fenrir snorts in such a way my palm is itching to slap his face.

"I need a shower, but as soon as Astara comes back I'll be ready." Taking a deep breath, I pull the sunglasses low on my nose and turn away from the wide stretch of windows so I can lock gazes with her. "Thank you for helping us out."

"You'd be smart to listen to him, Chicca." She smiles kindly for the first time, making her look younger than her appearance of mid-twenties. "He is a jerk, but he is not far off. Good thing I have stakes in this too, or you would've had only a memory of my magnificence to remember me by." Winking, she glides to the open doors. "Let's go wolf. I have no time to waste. This perfection doesn't come easy, so I have grooming to do."

I watch her leave, her heels snapping sharply on the marble tiles. Leo throws beefy over his shoulder, following behind her shirtless and barefoot not sparing us a single glance. Pushing my sunglasses up, I turn to Fenrir. He's stiff as a board, his fists clenching at his sides and the muscles in his jaw and arms jumping. Opening and closing my mouth a few times, I blow out a breath.

"I need a shower," mumbling under my nose, I search the area for the bathroom.

"Hellion." His word is strained, but I've had enough drama for the day.

"Look Fenrir, I get it. You and Myst have history and that's something I'd like to stay as far away from as possible. I have enough of my own shit to deal with. But don't try to fuck up a chance that could be the break we need just because you have your panties so far up your ass they're cutting off the blood flow to your brain." Chewing on the inside of my mouth, I look him up and down. "Alex will not expect anyone from the academy to show up. Remember? We talked about this. He predicts your moves, plus he has enough moles inside to know that nobody is going. This is something I can do, a wild card he won't see coming."

He gives me a sharp nod and flings his hand to the side in an invitation to walk with him. I keep my mouth shut while he guides me through a hallway into a stunning bedroom as large as my apartment back in Sienna. My brain is mush, so I don't pay attention to anything apart from the second open door leading to a bathroom.

"I'll be back," Fenrir murmurs, closing the door behind me.

Chapter Ten

I stand under the scorching hot spray until my skin prunes and my feet can't hold me up anymore. Surprisingly, I think about nothing. Not one stray thought enters my brain until I turn the water off and exit the shower, a cloud of steam following in my wake. The mirror fogs while I stand dripping water all over the soft rug under my feet. In a daze, my eyes land on the pile of dirty clothing I left on the ground. Thankfully there is a plush robe hanging on the back of the door because no way am I putting the same outfit on. I'll walk around naked first. That will give Fenrir an aneurism I'm sure.

Twisting my hair in a rope, I squeeze out the excess water before snatching the robe and wrapping it around me. The soft fabric swallows me whole, but the moment Zoltan's scent fills my nostrils my knees give out and I drop on the floor. With trembling hands, I pull on the fabric and bury my nose in it, breathing him in. Is he alive? Is he hurt? What are those monsters doing to him while I'm here getting ready to play at dress up?

It should be me there, not him.

I fight hard against the tears that are trying to come. The time for crying is long past. It won't help Zoltan or me anymore. Now it's time to keep my shit together and do something right for once in my life. Everything that's been bothering me since they took him becomes crystal clear in my mind. I know exactly what I'm going to do. Roberti thinks he is too smart. Two can play his fucked-up game. I'll lift my middle finger to him and the Board at the same time. A girl can't ask for more than that.

A soft knock comes from the other side of the closed door. When I don't answer it comes louder, then the door swings open revealing Fenrir's panicked face. His eyes flick around before they lock on me where I'm crumpled on the floor, Zoltan's robe pushed under my nose.

"Francesca." Rushing in, the Fae scoops me up. "I shouldn't have left you on your own."

"Right." Snorting, I wiggle so he can put me down. "Because nothing says awkward like you giving me a bath."

"You are not well." Ignoring me, he walks to the large bed and places me gently on the edge. "When was the last time you fed?"

"We ate together." No way am I discussing blood with him right now. "I'm not hungry." My stomach decides now is the right time to make the loudest gurgling sound in the world just to call me a liar.

Fenrir cocks an eyebrow at me.

I glare.

With a sigh, he moves around the room, opening drawers and digging through them with such focus I expect him to come out with a hidden treasure. In the meantime, I see the bedroom properly for the first time. Everything is simple, organized, and clean, like no one has ever stepped foot here. Typical Zoltan. His scent all over the robe tells a different story. The silky, dark gray sheets on the bed do too, but I stop thinking about it when a claw grabs my heart as if trying to wrench it out of my chest.

"Here"—Fenrir thrusts something in front of my face— "put these on for now."

I have to lift my arm up and wiggle my hand out of the sleeve before I can take the clothing he is giving me. I unfold it to see dark blue pajamas with a button-down top. Without a word, he walks out of the room and leaves me to dress. I don't want to stay here smelling Zoltan on everything around me, so I dump the robe and pull them on. The bottoms keep falling to my ankles, so I kick them off. Following Fenrir's example, I open a few drawers to find running shorts and other sportswear in one of them. Pulling on a pair of shorts that I cinch tightly at my waste; I grab the sunglasses from the bathroom and wander off in search of the Fae.

He turns around looking right at me the moment my bare feet enter the open-spaced living room. He must've cleaned up all the blood, water, and other bodily fluids while I was in the shower because everything is spotless. Waving me to sit on the couches, he comes out from behind the slab of marble separating the kitchen from the rest of the apartment.

Holding a glass of blood like a ritualistic chalice to be presented to the gods, he offers it to me. "You want to face Alexius tonight, you will drink this, Drake."

I shut my mouth with an audible click.

Tucking my legs under me, I sink in the soft leather and take the glass between my hands. Fenrir looms over me until I take the first sip, then he settles next to me stiff as a board. Sometimes I wonder how his spine doesn't snap from standing that straight. I gulp the warm blood while eyeing him over the rim. I can see a lecture coming so I wait.

"I can't protect you there, Drake." Staring at the large black screen of the TV, he sighs. "The moment Alexius catches a glimpse of me he will be gone … if he shows up at all."

"I'm not really a damsel if you haven't noticed." Licking the few drops still lingering on my lower lip, I lean in to place the glass on the low table. "Why are you so hell bent on protecting me anyway? I understand the need for you to make sure I don't end up a blood mare for Roberti, but this?" Waving a hand in his stern face, my cheeks puff out in frustration. "This is obsession, not duty, and it certainly isn't a friend caring for a friend."

"Apart from Soren, you are the only other dragon blood known in existence." Turning to me, he rubs the back of his neck. "The oath I gave you yesterday was just a confirmation to you. I made that oath centuries ago when I chose to join the academy. Your bloodline doesn't make you a shifter, but it's strong enough that regardless of you being a half blood, it trumps any other genetics. It makes you the most unique being in all the realms."

I blink at him.

"I still don't understand how your father managed to hide what he is, but I have a suspicion Soren had something to do with it." His nostrils flare. "When dragons decided to leave and retreat to a realm only known to them, they still honored their bond to the Fae that were loyal to them to the very end. Only one bloodline was given the power of having dragon magic—or as some call it, dragon soul—in their veins. Your father comes from that lineage does, and so do you. At present, you and Soren are the only connection we have with the dragons. We can't lose that."

"Okay." Dragging the word out, I still don't understand why he needs to be so uptight.

"If we lose the dragon bloodline, we lose our connection to the dragons. Their magic is holding everything together. My own realm, Sienna, and other realms. It'll all collapse on its own if that bond breaks. And that's not the worst of it." Taking a deep breath, his gaze flicks on mine. "Without that connection, all the wards that keep the old gods out of our worlds will be void."

"The book." Ice replaces the blood in my veins.

"Now you see why I don't want you anywhere near this gala?"

"I will not hide while Zoltan suffers." A lump forms in my throat, choking me. "I understand how important it is for me to keep breathing. Trust me, no one wants that more than I do, but you know as well as I that I'm his only chance. I'm hoping Roberti's need for me will keep Zoltan alive until we find him." Fenrir twists his mouth in displeasure. "I'm not planning on playing a hero, Fenrir. Because of me, he is being held hostage. I'm sorry to disappoint you, but even half-bloods have honor when it comes to things like this."

"You have more honor than most pure bloods I know."

"So, what's the problem then?"

"Zoltan will skin me alive if anything happens to you." Deflating, he plops back on the couch, his lips twitching.

"Neither you nor Zoltan are my keepers. This is what I've been doing my whole adult life, and I have no intention of stopping now." Playing with a button on my top, I admit out loud what I haven't voiced before. "I don't know how to be anything else. If I don't do what I'm doing, then I have nothing. I *am* nothing."

"There is a lot more to you Francesca Drake than you

know." Taking my fumbling fingers away from the button, he gives me a reassuring squeeze.

"Too bad I can't grow a tail and wings, huh?" My attempt to break the tension works and he grins at me. "If I could, I'd be flapping those suckers all over the place."

"I would expect nothing else." He looks so serious I giggle like an idiot.

"Are we getting a backup for tonight or will it be just us?" I watch him play with my fingers, turning them around in his hand. "If we do follow him, there might be a shit load of hunters there."

"That's why Leo left with just his pants on. He should be coming back here through the portal any moment." A long pause stretches before he peeks at my face. "I need you to promise me that at the first sign of trouble you'll be out of there, Drake."

"I want to kill that fucker more than anyone, but I'm not stupid Fenrir."

"I'll have to wait outside with our back up. I need your word."

"I promise I'm not going to do anything to get myself captured or killed."

"Thank you." His shoulders relax for a second before stiffening again. "About Myst …"

"Oh hell no." Snatching my hand away, I flap it frantically in his face. "Not my problem and I don't care. I'm not touching that subject with a ten-foot pole."

"Just be careful and watch your back. I don't trust her; she's unpredictable."

"Like me, you mean?" When he opens his mouth to argue, I laugh. "Don't worry Fae, I don't trust anyone … yet," I add when he gives me a pointed look to remind me of my promise to try.

"I come bearing gifts." The front door flings open and Astara waltzes inside with both arms full of bags. "I've forgotten how much fun it is to shop."

"Did you buy an entire store?" Jumping on my knees, I lean over the back of the couch to watch her spread the bags all over the place.

"No, but just because we are going there to find that piece of shit doesn't mean we can't do it in style." Triumphantly, she unzips one garment bag to reveal a simple but elegant black dress. "This right here is a show-stopper."

"You know you're not supposed to attract attention there, right?" If Fenrir's words are any dryer a cloud of dust will putt out of his mouth.

"I'm not going anywhere dressed in rags." Astara lifts her chin defiantly. "Besides, this is all on Zoltan's credit card. An early thank you from my dear brother for saving his ass."

I smile at her cheerfulness. I've been avoiding her out of guilt, thinking she is drowning in misery and blaming me for everything. Her liveliness might have something to do with the idea that we might find where Zoltan is tonight, but I'd like to think she knows her brother will handle whatever Roberti has set up for him while planning a good revenge in the process. If he asks for tips, I'll give him some of the ones that have been piling up in my head, too.

"Go dress." Throwing both hands in the air in defeat, Fenrir shoos us away. "Fates help whoever has to deal with both of you together. I'm glad I'll be on the sidelines." At my raised eyebrow, he grins. "You made a promise Drake. If you break it, I'll lock you up under the academy where you'll stay for a couple of decades to see the error of your ways."

Chapter Eleven

The city passes in a blur while I stare out the window. The long, sleek car Fenrir has picked for us has enough space to have a sleepover inside it. My hand glides over the leather absentmindedly while my gaze is focused on the reflection on the glass.

A stranger stares back at me.

Long, straight black hair falls around my shoulders. My skin is pale, which makes me look more like a vampire than a half blood. Dark eyes blink back at me with the lazy flutter of thick lashes. Astara has transformed me into someone I've never met before. Glancing at her from the corner of my eye, I'm still stunned how natural her transformation looks. Red locks are piled on top of her head with tendrils curling around her face. Every time she looks my way, I am startled by the light green color of her eyes. Wigs and contact lenses combine with a lot of make-up, making us strangers sharing this luxury car.

Hopefully it'll fool Alex as much as it does me.

"This is my stop," Fenrir murmurs, looking like his old

self when the car stops. "Remember to stay focused and no going off script. Especially you Drake."

I stare at him.

"We got this Fenrir," Astara assures him. "Just make sure we don't lose him if he senses something is off."

Fenrir keeps his gaze locked on mine. I hope he doesn't see all the thoughts jumbled there. Because do we? Do we have this?

I'm not so sure.

"I'll see you both shortly." Pulling his probing eyes away from my face, he slides to the door and cracks it open. "The glamour will hold, so just keep character." With that, he leaves the car.

I jolt slightly when the door closes with a thump.

"Will I react to the humans here like the first time I was around them?" Voicing my worry, I don't look at Astara. My hand still moves on the seat like I'm treading water, my fingers grazing the leather gently.

"The sigils will hold, Franky." Sinking further in the seat, Astara sighs while leaning her head back. "Nothing ever goes wrong when Fenrir does it."

Turning my left wrist, I pull the long sleeve of the dress to see the markings. Two sigils, their black lines twining together like vines, sit on my skin. I feel the magic thrum under my skin but I'm still nervous. I'm not like the rest of them. No one can be sure it'll work on me like it does on everyone else. I don't know how I feel knowing there is a possibility I can go crazy and attack everyone.

"Myst will meet us there?" Tugging the fabric to cover the markings, I take a deep breath.

"We are about to find out." She tilts her chin at the window.

The car stops in front of a building that looks like a

diamond bracelet, the mirrored walls curving around and twinkling in the city lights. Metal poles hold a glass façade jutting out and reaching for the street. Spotlights beam brightly at the entrance where humans who are dressed to impress move like they belong here. I curl my fingers in, the nails biting the skin of my palm to cover the nerves.

I can do this.

Zoltan's life is at stake.

Astara glides out of the car and steps to the side. My sweaty palm slips on the leather when I slide across the seat to exit. It's a good thing it's night and the harsh light is tolerable to my eyes. For some reason, my sight is a problem in this world of humans. Astara moves, almost prowling along the stretch of concrete to the open doors. I follow her lead, watching the emerald silk of her dress swish between her feet. It's similar to mine in length, and it looks painted on instead of like a fabric to protect us. Where hers is held by thin straps on her shoulders, the front draping all the way to her navel and giving a tantalizing glimpse of her breasts, mine is blood red, closed to my neck with long sleeves covering everything but my face.

That's the front.

A cool breeze sends goosebumps down my spine. My dress has no back, leaving my skin exposed all the way to my tailbone. The silk shifts with each step I take. A shiver rakes my insides. I don't like being exposed like this. Only the tight grip I keep on the clutch in my hand, my blades hidden inside and poking my palm, keeps me calm. I hope the burning between my shoulder blades is because Fenrir and Leo are watching me. I have a very bad feeling about tonight.

By the time I'm standing in a large circular room with a flute of champagne in my hand, I've already mapped out four exits. The back of the room is a dead end and the front is too exposed to do anything without being noticed. Astara is chatting with an elderly couple, giving the silver-haired lady kisses on both cheeks.

My gaze skips from face to face as I search for Alex.

"One o'clock, next to the woman with all the fur wrapped around her," Myst says from behind my shoulder.

I feel her approach at my back and it takes everything in me not to turn around. Sipping from my drink to cover my unease, I shift slightly so I can see her, my eyes moving to where she tells me Alex is.

"I see." The crystal in my hand cracks, so I force my fingers to unclench before it shatters.

The asshole is laughing at something the woman says, her hawkish face bathed in lust while she eats him with her eyes. I guess he has no qualms at using what he is to make humans drool over him. Her hand lifts, her long, pointed nails digging in the fabric of his tux where she grips his forearm.

"Who's that?" I ask Myst, but I stare intently at Astara in hopes that she'll notice and come closer.

"One of the Directors of the Board." Myst slinks closer, her head constantly moving from side to side like we are not both watching the vampire with rapt attention. "I'm not sure if it's just him being himself and gloating because he gets under her skin, or he has plans involving the Red Cross that we know nothing about. Either way, it's something to think about, for sure."

"I thought you worked for him. Shouldn't you know?" Astara finally says her goodbyes and heads our way.

"You'd think, right?" Myst answers a bit too cheerfully.

"Let's move closer, shall we?" Astara takes my elbow,

throwing her head back and laughing like I just told her the best joke of the century.

Every head in our vicinity turns to stare at her. I cringe internally. Didn't she say we shouldn't attract attention? My gaze jumps to Alex and I have to force myself to move smoothly without stiffening. He zones in on us like the predator that he is. My heart jumps in my throat when I realize he will recognize Myst. She has no glamour, at least not that I know of.

"He won't see her; she has her talents." Reading my panic, Astara grins at me like we are still having that funny conversation from a moment ago and pulls me along with her.

I'm too aware of Alex following us with his gaze.

"Well, you got his attention." Pushing the words through unmoving lips, I find it difficult to keep the smile plastered on my face. I've never been a good actress.

"Good." I have no time to ask what the hell she means by that when she stops me in front of a tall male with salt and pepper hair, his tux stretching over his broad shoulders.

"Governor, how very nice to see you this evening." Her purring, sultry voice makes the male turn to us immediately, which leaves the people talking to his back.

"Ms. Robins, how very nice indeed." The male beams at her like she's best thing after bread and butter. "You look as lovely as always."

I turn my head to give Myst a raised eyebrow. Her fake name is enough to make me almost swallow my tongue when I finally take a good look at the woman. Platinum hair stretched painfully in a high ponytail sits on top of her head. Her blue gaze is like sparkling oceans staring at me. Myst is almost a head shorter than me, so whatever her talents are, I wish she did my glamour. Then I see her dress. Or what should be a dress but it's more a turtleneck barely covering the juncture of her thighs. Her shoes only have a sole. Black fabric crisscrosses around her foot, moving up her ankle to her knee where it's tied into a pretty bow.

She winks at me.

"I see you haven't lost your charm since the last time I saw you." Astara jerks my head back to the conversation. "Oh, how rude of me. This is Ms. Atkins, a friend of mine that specializes in genetics. I was so excited to introduce you." Both Astara and the male turn to look at me.

I blink.

Oh shit, she's talking about me.

"A pleasure, Ms. Atkins." The governor lifts his palm.

I stare at his hand like it's a snake that will bite me. When my brain gets online again and I see he is waiting on me to take it, my arm jerks in his direction—the one holding a drink. Astara tips my elbow and champagne soaks the poor male's tux from chest to groin. I'm mortified, the blood curdling in my veins.

"Oh, dear." Myst gasps, snatching a tablecloth from the nearest table. "It's a good thing it's white." Giggling, she pats the governor with it, and by the reddening on his face and the shifting of his feet, she is probably groping him for all I know. He doesn't look like he minds.

"It's fine. It happens." He sounds strained but offers me a glazed smile. I frown at that. "It's one use only, anyway." He indicates his tux with a wave of a hand.

"I'm sorry," I mumble, still not understanding why these two are going off script and making a debacle that will surely give Fenrir a coronary.

"You are such a klutz." Astara swats my arm playfully. "It's a good thing she's smart. Her head is always in her research. She's a disaster waiting to happen, I tell ya," she says to the governor.

"Right." His smile is strained. It might have something to do with Myst still rubbing the fabric all over his stomach and hip area. "A geneticist you said?"

"It's an obsession of hers." Astara nods at me like she expects me to confirm this insanity.

Both her and the governor are watching me, so I swallow the lump in my throat.

"Yes." I sound faint, so I clear my throat. "I'm obsessed with …" What the hell am I supposed to be obsessed with? "Blood," I finish lamely, plastering a smile that must make me look constipated on my face.

Myst chokes.

I'm going to kill Astara after we get out of here.

"Well you've come to the right place then." The governor laughs heartedly, finally grabbing Myst by the shoulders and peeling her away from his body. She gives him a sheepish smile and bats her eyelashes.

I snort.

This is so fucking ridiculous I want to laugh. Imagining Fenrir's face when he sees this display just adds to the hysteria bubbling in my chest. Another ungraceful snort escapes me and the governor's lips twitch. That's all it takes. I burst out laughing, the three of them joining me a second later. Pressing my fingers under my eyes, I hope I don't mess up my makeup because of the tears about to spill over.

"What lovely company you keep, Governor." The voice from behind Astara is like a bucket of cold water being thrown over a burning fire. I'm the only one without a smile left on my face. "Mind if I join you?"

Astara shifts to the side and I lock eyes with Alexius. It's a herculean effort not to let my fangs drop and rip his throat out. On a good note, he doesn't seem to recognize any of us, so I guess the glamour holds after all. That doesn't help to slow the galloping in my chest, though. Seeing his nostrils flare and the glint in his eyes, I'm hoping he will assume it's from excitement and not murderous rage. The governor might yet see how obsessed I am with blood if I paint the walls here with this asshole's insides.

"Alex, of course, of course." The males shake hands, slapping each other's shoulders like old friends. I wish I know more about what is going on in the human world. "This is Ms. Robins; her charities are helping the Red Cross by providing shelters for orphans in many countries." Astara doesn't skip a beat as she places her hand in Alex's, offering him a broad smile. He lifts her knuckles to his lips, the light gleaming on his hair.

"Ms. Atkins is a geneticist I had the pleasure of meeting this evening." The governor's voice muffles in the background when Alex's gaze snaps to mine.

The magic in my chest uncoils at the intent look in his eyes, poking its head out and stretching my skin. I bite the inside of my cheek, careful not to draw blood. No way any glamour can cover up the scent of it to someone like Alexius. Both of us are frozen while waiting to see what reaction the other has. My ears are buzzing from the rushing of my blood. Can he see who I am? Does he know?

"Oh, it seems we lost the other lady." The governor breaks our staring match.

"Ms. Atkins's assistant must've gone to get us some drinks," Astara lies smoothly, not losing her smile.

Taking advantage of the break Astara gives me, I do my best to gather myself. *Come on Franky, you can do this,* I chant to myself, seeing that Myst is nowhere to be seen. I wish we can trade places.

"The speech will start soon." The governor throws an arm at a table positioned at the front. "Would you care to join me? A few people couldn't make it tonight, and it'd be a shame for me to sit there all alone."

"Of course." Astara folds her arm under his and they walk away, leaving me with asshole.

Well, this should be fun.

Chapter Twelve

"Shall we?" Alex cocks an elbow at me. It takes everything I have not to break it.

"Lead the way." I grin at him while keeping my limbs to myself.

"Very well." Chuckling, he tucks his hands in the pockets of his pants. "Have we met before, Ms. Atkins?" The way he says the name is enough for me to know he can tell it's bullshit.

"I don't think so." We walk next to each other, weaving through tables.

"You are correct." At my raised eyebrow, he gives me a cocky smile. "I would remember meeting such a stunning woman."

"I bet you make it a job to remember those." I want to slap myself for sounding snide.

"It would be a shame not to." His smile doesn't slip. He is too experienced at this verbal bullshit. I'm more of an all-hands-on-deck girl. Scratching his eyes out is a good example.

"So what do you do?" It doesn't escape my notice that he leads me across from Astara and the governor, pulling a chair out and waiting for me to take a seat. "What brings you here tonight?"

"I own a private network of blood banks across the world." Taking the chair next to mine, he twists his upper body and leans one elbow on the back of it. "We help the Red Cross when they have a shortage of a blood type, placenta, or whatever they may need."

My mind is already spinning from the implications of it. If what he says is true, what are Alexius and Roberti capable of when they have access to human blood like that? There is so much I don't know, but now is neither the time nor the place to start digging into it.

"You can place your purse on the table." He looks pointedly at the clutch I'm twisting between my hands in my lap. "I promise not to peek in it." He winks.

Like fuck I'm going to leave my blades out of my hand with a shark like him sitting next to me. I might be reluctant to do anything stupid with so many humans around, but I have no delusion that he doesn't feel the same. He will slaughter everyone here without blinking an eye.

"It's a habit." Leaning away from him, I cross my legs at the knee pointing the thin heel of my shoe at his shin. If he even twitches a muscle, I'm going to stab him with it to the bone. "To have something to do with my hands," I explain, slightly relaxing my shoulders.

It doesn't go unnoticed.

Alexius pulls out his phone, his fingers flying over the screen before tucking it back into his pocket. A woman walks up on the raised platform in front of us and I see it's the same lady wrapped in furs who was talking to Alex. She gives me the stink eye, glaring for a second before smoothing her features and plastering a wide smile on her face. Alexius doesn't seem to notice, his eyes boring into the side of my face like a gun pointed at my temples. I sit still while the woman talks, her voice droning on about stuff I neither hear, nor care about. A flash of platinum gets my attention. To the side of the platform I notice Myst, our eyes connecting for a second before hers flick to the ceiling, then she's gone. Alexius still hasn't looked away from me, so I lift my arm and rub the back of my neck. Rolling my head as if I'm trying to release the tension—which isn't far from the truth in any case—I tilt my face up and scan everything above me.

My heart skips a beat when I catch a glimpse of something white. The ceiling looks like a decoration on a cake, wide bends of red fabric the same color of my dress looping from the center to the corners of the room. I know I don't imagine someone moving up there. The blood is icing in my veins. Did Alexius bring hunters with him expecting trouble because he is being careful or is he onto us? I've been so uptight the entire day that a sense of calm washes over me at the idea I can stop pretending I'm something I'm not.

"Allow me." Murmuring under his breath, he pushes my hand away and replaces it with his own.

My whole body revolts the second his skin touches mine.

Instead of yanking away from him, I grind my teeth and reach for his emotions. If I am hoping to figure out whether he knows who we are or not, I'm disappointed. All I get from him is curiosity and confusion. Good, that means we are both confused. Everyone is paying close attention to what the woman is saying, an occasional round of applause thrown out for good measure. It gives me time to look around the room, staring at every shadow and corner. By the time I'm done, I know we will not be leaving this place the same way we walk in. So far, a handful of hunters are positioned strategically around the room and ceiling. I look at Astara across the table and she turns to me with a smile. It doesn't reach her eyes. Myst must've warned her as well.

I shift in my seat.

"Better?" Alex's voice is deeper and has a sharper edge to it.

"Much." Flicking his hand off my neck, I'm about to slide out of his reach but the trailing of his fingers down my spine freezes my movement.

Bile rises at the back of my throat.

"I have a feeling this is not the first time we've crossed paths, Ms. Atkins." He speaks under his breath, leaning so close to me I can feel his breath on my skin. "I have very good instincts, and I know you are hiding something."

My heart punches my ribs painfully, giving him the satisfaction of hearing it loud and clear. His chompers are too close to my neck for me to react like I normally would, which would be to punch him in the throat. Or stab one of my daggers through his eye. Wiggling my hips, I press the thin heel of my shoe to his leg, gliding it up his shin in what I'm praying to all the fates is a seductive manner and not what I really want to do, which is stab him with it.

Knowing who we are or not, I need to lure him out of here before shit hits the fan. All my instincts are on high alert, reacting to his predatory nature. Even if the glamour is holding, he still knows something is off. With the hunters not being subtle around us, no one stands a chance of surviving tonight, least of all the humans. *Fuck, Fenrir is going to kill me for this.* I can't hold back the groan when that thought pops in my head.

It works to my advantage.

Alex makes a noise deep in his throat, his palm pressing

firmly on the skin of my back. His other hand reaches for my thigh, moving slowly up my leg, his fingers squeezing my flesh. *Think, Franky, fucking think!* I scream inside my head. Steeling myself, I lean into him and tilt my face so our cheeks brush together.

"Let's get out of here." I sound breathless because adrenaline from the impending fight courses through me. My lips graze his ear and he shivers.

He yanks me out of the chair so fast I fall into his chest. Fast as lightning, not giving a damn who is watching him, he grabs the chair that is going to topple over and make a loud noise in the somewhat-silent space. Alex wraps his arm around my waist and practically drags me out of the room. I don't care what he does as long as we leave and the rest of his entourage follows. My chest is rising and falling fast, my hand crushing the clutch in my grip. The closed doors are my focus while he moves us towards them like a male on a mission. Heads turn to follow our progress, and I don't miss the pause from the woman on the stage.

Alex throws the doors open, swinging through them like a fury. My fingers fumble with the clutch so I can get to my daggers. His arm is like a metal vise around my waist, the fabric of his tux scraping over the bare skin on my back. The doors are closed with a kick of his foot, and before I can even formulate a thought about how to kill the asshole, he flings me against it, his mouth crushing mine in the same breath.

My body goes still as I let his tongue plunder my mouth, his hand groping my ass for way too long of a moment. His reaction stuns me, and by the time I snap out of it, my red dress is bunched at my hips and Alex is grinding his thick erection on me like he's a dog humping my leg. Since the hallway is empty I allow myself a second of insanity to actually pull my face away from his and laugh.

Eyes burning like coal, his lust sears my face. Thumping my head back on the door, I laugh harder. This is freaking insane. I was worried he knew something was up and would kill the humans, but the asshole was just horny and wanted a piece of ass. Well color me surprised. I feel sorry for his mate. At least the bitch deserves scum like him for getting so many people killed.

Five hunters materialize behind him. All humor leaves me in a rush. That's when I notice his thumb rubbing at my wrist. My entire body goes cold.

"You taste delicious, Francesca. It's funny how you thought your little glamour would fool me." His hips thrust harder against my thigh. The fact that he doesn't know Astara and Myst are here tells me the glamour fooled him plenty, but I don't tell him that. "I'll make sure to tell Zoltan you enjoyed every second that my tongue was inside your mouth." I stand stunned while he runs the tip of his nose along the side of my face. "I'll tell him about all the whimpering noises you make when I had you pinned against a door."

Our eyes lock and rage blasts my insides when I see the gloating on his face. The fucker wanted me to think he wasn't aware of who I was, and he succeeded. I only hope that Astara and Myst will have enough time to notice I'm gone for too long and follow us. There is no way I can fight my way out of this against Alexius and five hunters.

"I have a better idea." Grinning like the jerk that he is, he gives me a pat on the nose. "How about we tell him together?"

A flash of platinum catches my eye for a second behind the hunters. My fingers stop groping for the blades in my clutch. It might be stupid or a death sentence, but his gloating actually gives me an idea, and if that is Myst behind us, we might still get what we came for. Regardless of how he knows I'm wearing glamour, this actually may not be a bad situation, but only if Fenrir and Leo follow us and Astara realizes something is wrong. There are too many ifs, but still not a bad idea given the clusterfuck going on.

My clutch hits the floor, releasing a hollow thump on the tiles.

The grin stretches wider on Alexius's face.

He yanks the wig off my head and throws it to the side. Obviously, he doesn't give a shit who sees it. My own hair unravels, falling down my shoulders like a blanket. He watches my face for a long time, the red lipstick smudged on his lips like Joker's smile. I have a feeling he is not going to wipe his face until Zoltan lays eyes him. A pang pierces my chest at the thought of seeing Zoltan again.

"Let's go." Grabbing me by the arm, he jerks me away from the door.

I let him.

Striding through the long hall, he exits the building like a man that owns this world. Arrogance has been a downfall of many greater men. I can't wait to see the downfall of this one. With a bruising grip, he drags me towards a black car similar to the one we used to get here. It's so quiet outside, like the city itself is holding its breath in wait of what will happen next. I can feel probing eyes on the back of my head. Keeping my face down, I hide it with my hair. Fenrir is watching and he will follow. I have to believe that.

"Get inside," Alex snaps in disgust, throwing me inside the car.

I giggle, sprawling ungracefully on the leather seat before I lift myself and lean my back on the opposite door.

He glares at me when he folds in half to follow me inside, slamming the door closed as soon as he takes his seat. The car lurches forward, sliding between other vehicles passing on the street. A pissed-off driver honks long and loud before the sound grows distant behind us.

"This turned out better than I expected," he tells me conversationally.

You have no idea, I think to myself, keeping my mouth shut.

Chapter Thirteen

"We have a tail." The glass panel slides down just enough so we can hear the driver speak.

"Lose it." Alex is scowling at me.

The car jerks harshly to the left, the handle of the door digging in my ribs. Alexius doesn't move an inch, and it's like his ass is glued to the seat. The blaring of the horns and outraged screams of the humans create a background noise to match the frantic beating of my heart. My ankle is smarting because my stupid shoes made me twist my leg wrong when he shoved me inside the car. Grinding my teeth, I stay silent, hoping beyond hope that he will do the same.

I'm not that lucky.

"I assume that useless prick got himself caught?" Alexius asks, his voice betraying the annoyance he feels. "Is the book here or back in Sienna?" He yanks my arm to straighten me when I don't answer him.

"If you asked Zoltan, he would've told you I like it

rough like that. It's not going to work." I grin crazily at him. Maybe I shouldn't poke him, but I can't help it.

My head hits the window hard when he backhands me. My ears ring from it, but thankfully the car is still jerking left and right as we weave through traffic, so his hit doesn't come as hard as it can.

"We will have plenty of time to see how you like it, Francesca." Dread claws at my insides from the tone of his voice. "I'll make sure Zoltan is there to watch."

"You say the nicest things," I purr at him, swallowing a mouthful of blood from biting my tongue hard enough to feel it split on the side. "We will make sure your mate is there, too. I can teach her a thing or two, the poor girl."

My lungs protest at the lack of air when he grabs me by the neck, his fingers digging in my skin. Tears blur my vision, dark spots dancing at the edges of my eyes. I still manage to smile at the anger reddening his face.

"Do not mention my mate." He snarls in my face.

"She must be a lousy fuck if any female can get you worked up like I did." With great effort, I choke out the words. Strands of my hair are caught on my lashes, distorting his face even more.

His fingers tighten to a point where I'm about to pass out. It's really stupid to be unconscious around any of them. I should learn how to keep my mouth shut. At the last moment, he throws me away from him. Gasping, I suck in gulps of air and rub at my chest. It hurts like a bitch to breathe, but the air entering my lungs is the sweetest thing I've ever tasted.

Curling up in my corner, I tuck my head down and pretend to cower just so I don't do any more stupid things. Like talk for example. No one appreciates my sarcasm, which is kind of sad. In the back of my mind, I'm aware that my train of thoughts is not normal. I should be freaking out or fighting my way out of this damn car, but the idea of being where Zoltan is no matter the circumstances pulls stronger. I know Fenrir will find us. His magic is somehow tied to mine because of the oath. Even if he loses sight of Alexius, he will follow me. I have no doubt about that.

We leave the city behind, the lights diming until the inside is only bathed in the glow from the phone Alexius holds in his hand. A frown lines his forehead as he reads something on it, then his fingers move in a blur to type his response. I watch from the corner of my eye, letting my hair give me the cover to observe him. That same danger from our first meeting wraps as around him like a cloak. They all must have a secret I don't know about. Otherwise, any human with a bit of self-preservation won't be comfortable around any of them.

The car slows down and I mush my face on the window to see why we are stopping. Tall iron gates with a small, one man post to the side are closed and look ominous. The lights of the car don't penetrate the darkness so I can't see what's behind them. A hunter walks out of the post approaching the driver's side with his hand hovering over a dagger as long as my forearm that's strapped on his hip. Their voices are muffled but he moves back inside his station, and a second later the gates swing open. My eyes connect with the hunter's soulless ones through the window when we pass him.

A long, winding road leads us to a large mansion with jutting roofs and manicured lawns. The gravel crunches under the wheels of the car when it follows the roundabout driveway with a huge fountain in the middle. A statue of a woman with leathery wings and talons for feet stands on top of two lions whose mouths are open in a roar. Water gushes out of them. A crown made of some sort of bones is sitting on top of her head and the mane of her hair is made to look like the wind is playing with it. Dread chokes me just looking at it.

The car stops and my neck hurts from craning it to stare at the fountain. Something about the image of the woman prickles the back of my mind, causing my magic to swirl in my chest. I forget all about it when I'm yanked out of the car like luggage no one wants to carry.

"Move." Alexius shoves me ahead of him and my ankle twists again.

Flailing my arms, I manage to stay on my feet, but I do kick off the damn shoes, flipping them into the trimmed bushes and getting a grim sort of satisfaction for messing up their perfect shapes. Sharp rocks stab my bare feet, but I ignore the pain and keep my eyes on the set of stairs leading to a covered porch and double doors. I'm still on the second step when the doors swing open, a hunter holding them ajar for us. I should feel fear or something—anything really— from being in their midst. I don't. Instead, I'm impatient to see Zoltan.

"Drake!" Roberti walks out of a room and closes the door behind him, a wide smile stretching his face. "I knew you'd see reason."

I've either gone insane or there is something seriously wrong with him. I've known Roberti for most of my life. He's always been an asshole with no time for anything that doesn't interest him. Regardless of any of that, he's always been a very good-looking male, true to his demigod genes. The male standing in front of me looks sick. He still has his broad shoulders and trim waist, but the skin on his face and hands looks like it's graying. Dark circles form smudges under his eyes and his cheekbones jut out like bones sticking out of his face. The chocolate color of his eyes is pitch black, and it swallows his pupils to make them invisible.

It's unnerving as fuck.

"Andrius." Swallowing a lump the size of a fist in my throat, I search his face. There is no trace of the male I knew in Sienna there. "Nice place you have here."

"She didn't come for a visit," Alex spits from behind me. "She thought she'd trick me with glamour and follow me here." Roberti's gaze snaps to Alex over my head. "We still don't have the book."

"She just needs the proper motivation to see what's good for her." An insane glint enters Roberti's eyes, and it curdles my blood. "She'll bring the book herself after that."

"Well"—Clapping my hands like an excited child, I beam at Roberti—"it was great seeing you." Angling my body so I can slink around Alex, I keep them both in my sights. "Now that I know you're doing great; I'll just be on my way. See you around."

I bump into something and an ornate vase I don't notice shatters into tiny pieces on the floor. For a moment I wonder why Roberti and Alex are not trying to stop me. Instead, they're watching me like I'm an exhibit in a zoo. How odd. But when I feel the cold kiss of metal on my bare spine, I no longer wonder. I hate this stupid dress. The sharp tip of the blade presses harder onto my skin but doesn't break it. Alex smirks at me and murder burns in my chest. I'm going to wipe that look off his face if it's the last thing I do.

"You want to walk yourself or should I help?" Alex gloats, pointing to the right of the open grand foyer.

"I'll walk." Lifting my chin, I clench my fists.

"You had fun I see." Roberti chuckles at Alex as I walk

between them in the direction the asshole wants me to move.

"Ah yes." I can feel their eyes on me, the short hairs on my neck standing on end. "I'm looking forward to telling Zoltan all about it. You've been missing out all those years. She tastes delicious."

They keep chuckling but I ignore them both. I know Alex is trying to provoke me, and I'm also aware it'll work soon enough, but at least I'll try and pretend I'm not bothered by it for now. *Just play along until the rest get here,* I tell myself. Neither Roberti nor Alex knew I would pop up in that gala like some jack in the box. No matter how much security they have in this place, our chances are still good.

I hope.

I stop in front of a plain door, all the colors and decorations of this place just a blur around me. My mind is too busy to pay attention to anything that doesn't have a heartbeat. So far, only six are beating on this floor and that includes the two morons behind me and my own. Alex leans around, opening the door and brushing his chest against my arm. I don't flinch, although I really want to. Stairs lead into darkness that's gaping at me like the mouth of a hungry beast. Not giving myself time to freak out, I start going down.

They stand at the door until I'm almost covered in the darkness, then one of them flicks a switch and yellow light brings everything to life. I wish for the darkness again, but it doesn't come. The room is not too large, just gray floors and stained walls. I don't want to think about the cause of the dark patches on the yellowing paint. Iron bars separate one corner from the rest of the barren room to create a cage. In the middle of it, chains hang from the ceiling. The metal clasps that would normally hang at the end are clasped tightly over Zoltan's wrists. His arms are stretched painfully above his head. His knees are bent where he hangs limply like a doll his chin pressed tightly to his chest. A pool of blood glitters in the yellow light, a dark mirror under his feet.

I can't breathe.

A vise just like the ones around Zoltan's wrist squeezes my chest. Even my heart is stuttering because it's unable to thump properly. I stand frozen, too afraid to breathe in case I can't hear his heartbeat. I can feel Alex and Roberti coming down and getting closer, but I can't get my feet to move. Apart from their hearts and the stutter in my chest, I hear nothing else. Cold sweat drenches my body, the silk of the dress sticking to the skin between my breasts and on my belly.

I hear one slow *thump.*

"He is alive," Roberti says casually, like he is talking about an object instead of a person.

I say nothing, forcing my feet to move closer to the iron bars, my nails digging in the skin of my palms to hide the shaking of my hands. *He is alive, stop freaking out. He is alive,* I chant in my head while standing across the bars from Zoltan. I don't know what else to do.

"You expect me to say thank you for keeping him alive?" My voice sounds hollow to my own ears.

I can't look away from Zoltan. His hair is dirty, clumped in places from dried blood. The shirt he is wearing is ripped to shreds, making all the cuts and bruises visible on his skin. For the wounds to still be open and trickling blood, he must be almost drained. He would've healed otherwise. I would do anything to see him lift his head right now and smirk at me. Or even say something arrogant to piss me off. Anything really. Seeing him like this kills something inside me. I can physically feel some integral part of who I am break apart and turn to dust.

It doesn't even hurt.

"Should we wake him for the reunion?" Alex sounds too excited about the idea. He can't wait to show the smudges of the lipstick still on his face, I bet.

I'll take that. I'll take Zoltan being angry and even hating me just to see him look at me. I need to see those blue eyes open, to know that he is really alive. A metal stick pokes between the bars and Alex jabs the end of it in Zoltan's chest, sending sparks of electricity everywhere. I'll break my teeth from grinding them so hard, but I stay still as I wait for Zoltan to lift his head. His body jerks violently. *Look at me,* I beg silently in my head. *I'll do anything for you to look at me.*

The chains snap tight and Zoltan throws himself forward.

Red blazing eyes glare at my face with no recognition of who I am. Saliva drips from his fangs as he snaps his jaws at me. With veins bulging on his neck and arms, he strains against the chains to get to me. Not because he missed me, and not because he is angry at me. No, this is worse.

He is feral.

Chapter Fourteen

Roberti and Alex left a while ago, locking me in here with Zoltan. They got tired of gloating and laughing at my face. I couldn't do anything but stand staring at those red eyes while he snarled and growled at me.

His beautiful face is contoured in hatred and bloodlust even now.

Curled up with my knees hugged to my chest, I keep watching him. Even moving to the furthest corner doesn't stop him from yanking on his chains, his hunger to see me dead stronger than anything else. I know it's not him. It's that poison they put in his blood, but it doesn't make it easier to see. Tears trickle down my face and I poke at my eyes to get the damn contact lenses out.

"This is all my fault." Flinging the vile thing that was stuck to my eyeball, I let anger replace the hopelessness trying to drag me down. "I should just let you kill me and be done with it."

It might be my imagination, but it looks like the sound of my voice is slowing him down. The moment I look into his eyes he snarls, almost pulling his arms out of their sockets with a vicious snap of his jaw. I cringe. Yup, just wishful thinking.

"Here I was, dying little by little inside just thinking of you finding your mate." Blabbing out the first thing that comes to mind, I rub at what's left from the sigils on my wrist. Better talk than think. "You can't just turn feral after kissing me senseless and making all those promises, Zoltan."

A lump chokes the rest of the words and more tears trickle down my cheeks. I can't even think of facing Astara after she sees her brother like this. And she will see him. No way will I have the heart to kill him before they get here. I'll let Zoltan rip out my throat first.

He calms down when I'm quiet, but those red eyes are glued to me like he is worried I'll disappear if he blinks. It's unnerving to say the least. My sniffles while I jerkily swipe the tears from my nose and chin is the only sound. The walls must be reinforced down here so no one can hear the screams. My gaze traces the stains on the walls, more to avoid looking at Zoltan than anything else. I feel numb. I talk a lot of shit to his face, but I can admit to myself that the moment he dies, I'll die with him. Maybe not physically, but the numbness is taking root inside my soul and preparing me for the inevitable.

The most fucked-up thing about the whole situation is I don't see how I could've done things differently for a better outcome. I give them all so much crap about losing one person for the good of many, yet I do the exact same thing.

Snorting, I rub a hand over my face, grimacing when I see all the black and red paint on it. There goes the makeup. Maybe Zoltan is snarling at me because I look like my face is melting or something. Avoiding his gaze, I tilt my head back on the wall and close my eyes. The sigh passing my lips sounds like it's wrenched from the bottom of my soul. I still can't stop crying, so the tears roll out of my closed lids and fill my ears.

"What a fucking mess." My shuddering whisper fills the space between us.

I'm not sure how long I sit like this. My muscles are cramping from hugging my knees like someone will take my legs if I release them when I hear the door at the top of the stairs open. I roll my head to the side, waiting to see who will come to torment me first. I'm surprised they last this long before coming here to gloat. My heart punches painfully against my ribs when the feet of a hunter pad silently down the stairs. My body stiffens at the first sight of the white boots. When the dagger dripping with black sludge makes an appearance, I'm on my feet faster than I can blink. The hunter stops at the bottom of the stairs still watching Zoltan.

Fear claws at me with the idea of them turning me feral as well. With both me and Zoltan out of our minds, Roberti doesn't need to fight the Daywalkers when they come. The two of us will do the work for him. He wants us to kill our own. The magic inside me rages at the thought and I pounce on the hunter.

Grabbing the wrist of the hand holding the dagger, I wrench it behind the hunter's back at the same time as my elbow connects to his face. The hunter twists around, ducking to follow the arm I'm twisting and swiping my feet from under me. I drop on my back with an *oomph*, taking him down with me. No way I'm letting go of that damn dagger. Holding the arm with the blade as far away from me as I can, I scissor my legs, flipping my body over the hunter. Straddling his chest, I cock my arm to knock him out.

"Chicca, I told you I don't swing this way." Myst groans, jerking her head to the side just in time for my knuckles to shatter against the concrete.

Stars burst behind my eyes from the impact.

"I'm so glad that wasn't my face." She snickers like there is something funny here. "I'd be really unhappy if I needed to rearrange my features."

"What the fuck is the matter with you?" Hissing at her, my upper lip curls over my fangs.

"You and the hunk are quite the couple right now." She blinks innocently at me. "What, with all those fangs and snarls. Pretty hot, I promise." I can see why Fenrir is down-right rude around her.

The woman is insane.

"What are you doing here?" Pushing off her, I get to my feet, not offering her a hand up. "Are the others with you?"

"It'll be a while before they get here." Jumping up, she yanks the covering off her face. "It takes longer when you have to coordinate a lot of people." One of her shoulders twitches in a shrug. "That's why I work alone."

"So, what's the plan?" I notice she closes the door behind her, which tells me she snuck down here. Crazy or not, she's very good at this.

"I came to check on you first." She walks closer to Zoltan, who is going berserk from her nearness. I pretend not to notice. "This might be a bit of a problem." Her head tilts this way and that, and she whistles low when he snaps his jaws at her.

"You think?" snapping, I take a deep breath to calm myself. Killing her will not help me get out of here. I must remember that.

"Just a blip in the plan, Chicca." Waving my anger

away, she keeps studying Zoltan, who is focused on me again. "I see."

"Wanna share with me what it is that you see?" Grinding my teeth, I fight the urge to cry and rage at the same time. "Because from where I'm standing, we lose no matter what."

"What is it with you people and always looking at the worst-case scenario?" Myst turns to me incredulously, like I'm the one sounding crazy here.

Leaning forward and getting in her face, I glare. "He is feral," I tell her slowly, as if I'm talking to a dumb person, "if you didn't notice. That's what the red eyes and snapping jaw mean."

"You don't say." If her words were any drier, they would've crumbled off her lips. "I'm going to scout the house to see what numbers we are dealing with." Like a switch, her attitude flips. "I'll have the information for the others when they get here. You stay here until I come get you. We don't want to have to rescue you from Roberti or Alex if we can help it. And do me a favor, would you?" When I just stare at her, she smiles. "Kill anything that comes down here unless it's me."

She is looking at something over my shoulder while she talks, and my head moves so I can see what has her attention. Myst grips my jaw and she jerks my face to her.

"Deal?" Her smile is as sweet as poison.

Do not kill the woman until you get out of here, Franky, I repeat many times in my head until I can trust myself to speak. "Deal." I squeeze the words out.

"Brilliant." She grins widely before dancing around me to head for the stairs. I breathe through my nose to calm myself. "And Chicca," she calls from the top of the stairs in a whisper-yell, a crazed glint in her eyes. "Don't have too much fun without me."

I have no time to even form a coherent thought before she flicks a couple of switches on the wall and slinks out of the door, locking it behind her. The sound of metal grinding and chains dropping on the ground numbs my brain. My eyes are about to pop out of their sockets and that's when I feel the hot breath ruffling the hair on the right side of my face.

"Fuck." I breathe.

Zoltan is standing right behind me. My skin is pebbled with goosebumps from fear and from his nearness. The heat from his chest is like a furnace burning the skin on my back. I'm too afraid to even take a deep breath so I don't trigger him. Sweat beads on my hairline and upper lip just knowing he is ready to drain every drop of blood from me. To make matters worse, my body is responding to him, the scent of my arousal mixing with the burning stench of my fear.

And he can smell it all.

Instinct kicks in and I jerk my head back, headbutting him. The crunch of bone when my skull connects to his nose hurts me more than Zoltan, I'm sure. Spinning on my heel, I push him as far away from me as I can. He stumbles back but doesn't fall. Now that I'm facing him, I can see Myst—the idiot that she is—has lowered the bars of the cage, releasing him to kill me. She isn't here to help us. I'm stupid for thinking otherwise. Either way, I'm happy I'll be dead before I have to listen to the Fae lecture me.

Zoltan lunges for me, his arms outstretched and fangs bared. I send him flying to the opposite wall with a round kick, ripping the bottom of my dress in the process. He hits the wall hard, dropping on all fours and shaking his head as if to clear it. I can feel my magic pushing to the surface to come to my aid and I give it free reign. Zoltan's face snaps to mine, his gaze locking on mine just as my vision starts shifting to bring all the colors around me to life. The magic shrinks back, disappearing like it never existed. I blink stupidly at him until I realize he is using his mind control to force my powers to recede just like he forced Argoz to shift back at the academy.

I see his shoulders stiffen, the muscles on his arms and neck bunching, and I know he is about to pounce. All my powers, everything I've hated but need this very moment, desert me as I stare at my death in the face of a male I want to kiss instead of kill. The face of a male I will let drain me of blood because I'm not strong enough to be the one to take his life. He comes at me full force, the impact of his chest hitting mine pushing all the air out of my lungs. My back hits the wall behind me and my vision dims when my skull cracks against it. I feel the warm blood wetting my hair and the flare of red in Zoltan's eyes. My arm lifts to cup his cheek just as his fangs sink into the skin of my neck. My tears splatter the side of his face as he takes mouthful after mouthful, gulping it greedily.

Zoltan pressing me to the wall is the only thing holding me upright. My knees are weak, and if he moves, I'll drop on the floor. Not that he has any intention to move. My heart is beating sluggishly in my chest, like a butterfly with broken wings attempting to fly. Out of nowhere, power surges through me and flings Zoltan to the other side of the room. I hit the ground at the same time as him. The cold concrete mushes my face as I stare unseeing, only a pinprick of light in front of me. Stupidly, I think I hear Zoltan calling my name, but I have no energy to even blink. My head is lifted off the ground and something warm trickles down my throat. I swallow on impulse and everything goes dark.

Chapter Fifteen

Groaning, I swat the hand away that's insistently slapping my face. It doesn't hurt but it stings and it's annoying. When that doesn't help, I roll tucking my chin as close to my chest as I can. A hand grabs my shoulder, yanking me to my back and a loud slap echoes in my ears. My cheek is burning.

"No … nope! Wake up, Chicca." I hear Myst through the fog in my head. "No time for napping." She keeps slapping my face.

"Stop that." With a hiss, I jerk my legs up, flipping around and ending in a crouch.

"Okay, good." She grins at me. "You are still kicking."

"I'm going to kill you now." Everything comes back. She locked me in here while releasing Zoltan from the chains.

"Whatever for?" Myst looks taken aback. "I admit if I knew you were this stupid I would've stuck around, but all is good now. I got the hunk stashed back."

I blink at her.

Leaning down to get closer to my face, her smile slips away. "I thought you are smart and would use your brain,

Chicca. All you needed was to knock him down and feed him some blood. He was drained enough to be an easy job for you." Shaking her head in disappointment, she grimaces. "You were thinking with your vagina. How disappointing ... No male is good enough to die for just because he gets you all hot and bothered." Straightening, she rolls her shoulders while muttering under her breath. "Trust me, I know firsthand."

"What are you talking about?" I have to press one knee on the floor when my head swims and the room tilts. "You left me here so I'd turn feral, too. Your plan is not working ..." I trail off.

My head turns and I see Zoltan sprawled on the ground like someone dragged him there before raising the bars of his cage. Chills dance over my spine remembering the stuttering of my heart. I should be dead; Zoltan is not himself and there is no way he stopped to spare me on his own. All he wants is to kill and slake his bloodlust. His eyes tell that story.

My eyes flick back to Myst.

"You thought I wanted you dead." It's not a question and her voice is flat.

I just stare at her. Still dressed in the white clothing of the hunters, she unnerves me with those eyes of hers. There is something behind them, lurking and watching me through her. Having the same thing inside myself, it shouldn't disturb me ... but this is different. I'm not sure she's even aware of it.

"If I wanted you dead, I would've killed you a while ago," she points out and I almost laugh. "I don't need anyone else doing my dirty work. When I want you gone, you'll know it." Her narrowed eyes tell me she is completely serious.

Standing up and practically looming over her petite frame, I take stock of my body. With how much blood Zoltan took from me, I shouldn't be able to open my eyes, much less move around. Ignoring the narrowing of Myst's eyes, I scan the room. It's just the two of us here and Zoltan still unconscious behind iron bars.

"You gave me your blood." I search her face but this time she finds everything else fascinating and won't look at me.

"We don't have time for sentimentalities, Chicca." Wrapping that attitude around her like a cloak, she cocks her hip. "It's just blood and I have plenty of it. We are here to mess those fuckers up. So, let's get on with the program, shall we?"

If I know anything in my messed-up life, it's that supernaturals guard their blood more than they guard their lives. Myst herself was the first to point out she doesn't like anyone chewing on her—as she put it so eloquently the first time I saw her. If I'm being honest with myself, I probably wouldn't offer my own unless it was for Astara or Zoltan. Which brings back the memory of him draining me an inch from my life with absolutely no recognition of who I am in his gaze. My questions for Myst can wait.

"Will he be okay?" Turning to Zoltan, my heart skips a beat.

He hasn't moved at all; the longer strands of his hair are plastered on his forehead and blood is smearing his face where I broke his nose. With a slack jaw, his lips are parted and his fangs are still extended, curling his upper lip slightly over them. Only the barely-there rising and falling of his chest tells me he is still alive. Alive, but not necessarily cured of being feral.

"He will be okay for now, as long as we don't let anyone

get through that door." Myst pulls my attention back to her. "Your backup should be here soon. While I was skulking around the mansion, I found out they didn't expect to have a fight on their hands today."

"We have a chance of getting out of here with minimal damage you mean?" Glancing at Zoltan, my stomach clenches painfully. "The rest of us, I mean."

"The hunk will be as good as new before you know it." Scowling at me, she watches me as if she's judging my sanity. I wonder about that myself at the moment. "You just make sure to bleed as little as you can and get your ass out of here."

"What about you?" At her glower, I chuckle. "I can feel your blood inside me, Myst. I'll take a wild guess and say you are not exactly a typical female either. I'm starting to think I should make sure you are out of here faster than myself."

"I made sure you lived." Before I blink, she's in my face, one dagger pressed tightly under my chin. "As payment for my generosity, you keep your opinions to yourself and you never mention this to anyone. Are we clear?" The blade presses harder on my skin, not breaking it but close to nicking it. "It never happened."

That thing inside her—whatever it is— is clearly visible and thrumming with eagerness. I can't decide if it wants me to pretend this hasn't happened or to shove her away so it can come out to fight. My own power finally stirs in my chest, excited at the prospect of facing something unknown. That's when her irises darken to swallow her pupils and two dark, bottomless pits meet my gaze. My insides shrivel and numbness spreads like wildfire through me.

"Crystal clear." The words pass through my unmoving lips.

"Cool." The switch in her personality is flipped just like that and she grins again. "We should maybe chain him up again just for pretense? If anyone sneaks in, they'll think it's nothing—"

A large boom shakes the ground and walls around us. We both stagger on our feet, arms jerking to the sides to keep our balance. Another explosion follows, and this one is stronger than the first. Dust and plaster rain over our heads as I turn to look at Zoltan making sure nothing falls on top of him.

"The cavalry has arrived." The drumming in my chest matches the excitement in Myst's voice, the giddiness of an upcoming fight spreading through me when I look at the eagerness on her face.

"They'll be here any second." My fingers twitch with the need for a weapon. "Roberti won't leave us on the off chance that we'll stay docile here."

"I think they'll be too busy to be able to check on you two right now." Rushing up the stairs, Myst presses her ear against the closed door. "That's not to say hunters won't be swarming this room." Turning to look at me standing at the bottom of the stairs, she gives me a once over. "I need to go check on things. You'll be okay?"

"I need a weapon." Shouts almost drown my words.

"You are a weapon, Chicca. Stop thinking what's right or wrong and just kill anyone that tries to walk through this door." She is still watching me like I might not be all there.

"I'll make sure I do that even if it's you coming back." Frustrated from her scrutiny and pissed off at myself for getting in a situation like this, I glare at her.

"If that's how I go, I deserve to be killed." A wide smile spreads across her face and she winks at me before slinking out the door.

The female definitely has some screws loose in her head. The house rocks again, sending me stumbling into the nearest wall. Right. I just need to make sure no one is left standing if they open that door. I can totally do this. My head jerks around the room in search of something I can use to fight before I stop myself. What in the worlds am I doing? Zoltan is safe for now, protected by the iron bars of his prison, and here I am looking for something to knock people out when I need to kill whoever comes to check on us. Perhaps Myst isn't far off the mark by thinking I'm stupid.

Grabbing hold of the banister, I pull myself to the side so I'll be seen when the door opens. Pressing my back to the wall, I glance down and frown at the stupid dress. Taking a fistful of fabric, I yank on it and tear it in half. Another hard pull and a long section falls to the ground, leaving me with just enough material to cover the tops of my thighs. At least I can use my legs without tripping on the damn thing.

Zoltan groans softly and my heart jumps to the back of my throat. If he is still feral there will be no hiding for me. I shiver at the memory of his snarls while he watches me with his red eyes. Luckily, he only twitches but stays down. Thumping the back of my head on the wall behind me, I try to clear it. *Get it together, Franky. You found him, now you just need to get the hell out of here. You can do this.* The pep talk helps steady my trembling hands. The deep breath I attempt to take gets stuck in my lungs when the door above me opens and two sets of feet beat a rhythm on the stairs.

My body jerks when a pulse of power bursts out of the center of my chest unexpectedly. It's never come like this before with no warning, and for a split second I wonder if that's because of Myst giving me her blood. Then the white clothing of a hunter comes into view and all thought leaves my mind.

I move.

With one hand still gripping the banister, I swing my leg and catch the hunter on the side of his head. He obviously doesn't expect it, his body hitting the opposite wall so hard his head makes a horrible cracking sound before he drops in a heap on the floor. I'm already moving, spinning around and coming face to face with the second one, who is standing frozen two steps from reaching the bottom.

His eyes narrow to slits, hatred burning in them.

The hunter throws his body at me so he can tackle me to the ground. His hands are empty of weapons, so I take advantage of it and, instead of fighting him, I slam both palms to the center of his chest. With a comical widening of his eyes, he tries to spin midair to avoid my grip but he only makes it easier for me. My knees bend slightly. As soon as my palms connect, I push with everything in me, twisting around while guiding more than flinging him over my head. His fingers latch onto my upper arms, but the gravity is working against him. I jerk him by handfuls of his clothing, swinging him right at the wall a few feet away.

Red blood splatters like a bucket of paint thrown at the yellowing plaster on the wall where his face hits it. My gut clenches tightly but the door is opening again and I turn to face the new threat. Roars and screams are much louder now that I'm not closed in where the reinforced walls hide them from me. What in fates name is happening out there? It doesn't sound like they aren't ready for a fight. There are way too many voices for it to be the backup Fenrir and Leo organized. Fear chokes me while I stare at the stunned hunter who is standing at the top of the stairs staring at me.

Pushing off the balls of my feet, I sprint up the stairs.

No way can I sit here waiting for them to come to me. My friends, the people I care about are probably dying out there. I don't want anyone to get near Zoltan but that doesn't mean I can't be outside that door helping them. I'll just stand guard in the hallway. All these thoughts zip through my head as I reach the hunter who is pulling a dagger from the small of his back. Horror stabs me in the chest for a second before I see there is no black sludge on the glinting blade. No potions for this asshole tonight.

Coming from below him gives me a chance to tuck my shoulder under his ribcage and barrel through the partly-open door while carrying his weight with me. Searing pain makes me grind my teeth when his hand slashes down to split the skin on my bare back. Pushing up, I fling him off me and down the long stairs, a pained shout and the thumping of his body rolling down the last sounds I hear before silence takes over. A quick look shows me he will not be getting up, not ever. His head is twisted in an unnatural angle after all, and there's no coming back from that.

With an internal shrug, I face the hallway.

It's chaos.

Chapter Sixteen

My fingers tighten on the doorframe when I bend my upper body to avoid the flying shuriken passing an inch from my face. The deadly metal star glints ominously in front of my eyes before hitting something to my right and shattering it. The air warms to dangerous levels, forcing me to take a step back until I'm inside the door. Poking my head out, I try to see what's going on.

My jaw drops.

A mage dressed in the academy uniform is standing in the middle of the hallway to my left. His arms are stretched in front of him, his hands moving in circles while his fingers twitch. Magic swirls around him like a tornado with each move he makes. Face intense with concentration, he ignores everything around him. A demon guard is spinning circles around the mage, his sword slicing the air and protecting both of them from the blades thrown in their direction. The mage stops his frantic movements, pulling both arms towards his chest just as the demon steps behind him.

The mage's hands fling outward and flames burst from

them like an inferno. The heat is so much I'm surprised my eyebrows are still there. I have to clutch the banister so I don't fall down the stairs when my foot steps back and only my toes find purchase. My heart jumps in my throat for a split second until I'm sure I'm not going down. The flames blaze like a rushing river for a long time, searing my lungs with each breath I take.

And then everything stops.

I blink at the blackened walls opposite me in stunned silence. What the hell just happened? I'm still stupefied when the mage and the demon jog in front of me, moving down the hall with somber looks on their faces.

"Drake." They both nod in my direction, not pausing for a single moment.

I've seen their faces before, but I don't know their names. I wasn't aware any of them were close to Fenrir or Leo. Peering out, I see their backs just as they round a corner and disappear from view. The hallway is burned to hell and three charred bodies are just a pile on the ground.

The sound of fighting comes from all sides, but here in my bubble of death where I stand with the stench of burned flesh, I find a moment of peace. I have no intention of letting anyone get close to Zoltan again, so I push the door open a sliver so I can catch any movement in the hallway. I breathe through my mouth, avoiding the cloying scent so I don't gag.

That's when I hear him.

"Ms. Drake, I suggest you get down here." Zoltan's voice is raspy, and it sends a thrill through my body, which is a stupid reaction considering the situation, but nothing is ever different when the vampire is around. I have accepted the fact that I'm a moron when it comes to Zoltan. I mean, the jerk nearly killed me, but somehow, he still has the balls to call me "Ms. Drake" again. Go figure …

Pressing a thumb and a forefinger to the bridge of my nose, I pray to stay calm and not start cursing him to hell.

"Now, Francesca." The authority in his deep voice stiffens my shoulders.

Nudging the door closed with my shoulder, I descend the stairs slowly, telling myself to stay calm and collected. My palms are already sweaty, and my stupid heart is making me lightheaded from how fast it's galloping in my chest. Goosebumps spread like a rash over my arms and legs when he growls impatiently. I guess I'm not moving fast enough for him.

Jerk.

"Look who's awake." I hate that I sound choked up and that tears blur his face for a second. "You have a nice nap?"

My chest feels too tight when his familiar blue gaze connects to mine. I find it difficult to breathe, but not because his eyes are narrowed on me and he looks furious. He is alive and back to his normal self. If anyone would've told me I'd miss his arrogant attitude, I would've told them they were nuts. Yet here I am fighting tears because he is glaring at me like he wants to throttle me for daring to keep him waiting a second too long.

I'm stupid, I know.

"Release me." His growl vibrates deep in my own chest, the order loud and clear.

The blood is still smeared over his porcelain skin, which makes him look terrifying when paired with the glow coming from his gaze. Dark strands of his hair are sticking out every which way, clumped in places where his fingers have pushed it out of his face. He should look ridiculous or like a murderer. A pure blood. My worst nightmare. Zoltan looks raw, wild and I've never seen him look more appealing. Everything I am reacts to him and it's completely out of my control.

He smirks.

Seeing that familiar tilt on one side of his full lips flipflops my insides and makes me sway where I stand across the iron bars. We stare at each other and the fight, the cage, the bodies ... all of it is forgotten. His gaze travels the length of my body and heats as it moves. Pebbles rise in its wake like he is physically touching me, at least until his eyes land on mine again. For a split second in time and space, it's just him and me. It feels monumental, but for the life of me I don't understand why. The glow in his eyes swirls and intensifies. His pupils pulse and stretch into shapes of the sun—something I've seen before and will never forget— spreading over his irises for a moment before retracting. I take a startled step back when they flip to the vertical slits I've seen in my own eyes before returning to his Daywalker shape.

The world bursts to life with colors I see when my own pupils change, the magic inside me thrumming through my blood. It vibrates like a deep purr of excitement or contentment, but I'm not exactly sure which. Zoltan cocks his head slightly, the quirk of his lips growing. It's there for a moment and gone the next.

"Release me," he repeats, taking a step closer.

"No."

"No?" One of his eyebrows crawls to an arch. It should look ridiculous, but it doesn't.

My knees go weak.

"Last time you were out of the cage you almost killed me." Which is the stupidest reason I can give him for not letting him out.

The truth is, I'm not sure I won't throw myself at him and cling to his body for dear life if the bars aren't there to hold me back. It takes everything in me to not crumple into a weeping, slobbering mess on the floor. I must be a good liar because he jerks back like I've slapped him, guilt and pain flashing through his gaze. My stomach clenches at the lie but I stay silent.

"I assure you, Ms. Drake, that I am myself." His shoulders stiffen and the heat in his eyes disappears. I miss it fiercely. "I would never harm you if I had control of my mind." He sounds like I needed reassurance of that. Which I don't.

I never did.

Since I'm back to being Ms. Drake and I'm good at ignoring the pain that stabs me in the heart from hearing it, I turn away from him. Keeping my spine straight, I walk to the switch Myst flipped to release the iron bars. I'm halfway there when the door above me flings open and two hunters rush down the stairs. They already have their weapons drawn, fortunately with no black sludge on the blades. We've had enough feral dealings for this century thanks to Zoltan. They don't need my unstable and unknown crazy added to the mix.

Both the hunters are large, closer to Zoltan's frame instead of Fenrir's tall and lean swimmer's build. If I wait for them to come down, they'll dwarf me and I'll be hard pressed to fight. But like most males large enough to look intimidating to a female, they'll underestimate my reaction. I know they expect me to take a step back ... or the fates forbid, flee.

As soon as the first one is close enough—thank you stairs and tight enough spaces to allow one sword wielding person at a time—I step into him instead of backing away.

The swinging of his arm goes over me as I lean into his chest and grab his forearm with both my hands. Slamming his back into the wall, I wrench his arm until it pops out of the socket, eliciting a girly scream of pain from his throat. The sword he holds drops to the hard floor with a clink from metal hitting concrete.

The momentum lifts his lower body, his legs hitting his friend who can't stop in time to avoid it. The second hunter hits the stairs and sprawls on his back, a grunt of pain rumbling his chest when his spine lodges against an edge. My head jerks back, slamming the first hunter in the face. The force rattles my brain for a second and bright spots dance at the edges of my eyes. Blinking fast, I do my best to clear them as quickly as I can. The second hunter doesn't stay down long. He scrambles to his feet, snarling at the same time.

Reaching for the fallen sword, my leg flips into a high kick and my foot connects with his chest. The hunter goes down a second time as I straighten with the sword clutched in my hand. Falling at my feet, the first hunter curls into a ball while clenching his messed-up arm to his side. Without overthinking it too much, I take the lesson Myst gave me seriously for the first time. The hunters are not trying to kill me because Roberti has a use for me. Otherwise, I would never have been captured in the first place; I would be dead. However, some of them may be killing my friends at this very moment, and that thought doesn't sit well with me.

The second hunter jerks his head up from where he is sprawled on the stairs and his soulless eyes send dread through the marrow of my bones. Swinging the sword over my head, I grab the hilt with both hands and crouch, stabbing the hunter at my feet through his neck and almost decapitating him. Blood sprays in an arch above his body covering my chest and face. I blink it out of my eyes, not taking my eyes off the second hunter.

With a roar he jumps at me. The two daggers he holds in his hands are as long as my forearm, and they slice the air in fast, jerky movements. My sword keeps them away from my body, the sound of metal hitting metal echoing and bouncing off the walls in the close-knit space. He kicks out, swiping my feet from under me the second he corners me at the bottom of the stairs sending my weapon cluttering away. My back hits the ground, the air exiting my lungs with a loud *oomph*. The hunter jumps a foot in the air, his knees curling and his arm lifting over his head. The dagger aimed at my chest is coming too fast. My only hope of stopping it rests in flinging my forearm across my breasts.

My vision dims from the searing pain when the blade slices through the muscle of my forearm, the sharp tip still managing to stab me in the boob. I've never been this happy to have the round globe of muscle sticking out of my chest. *Saved by a boob.* I laugh in my head, which I know deep down is my irrational brain's way of protecting me from the pain. *Not many can say that.* A moment later, hysterical laughter bubbles out of me, and it's so loud that even the hunter is taken aback.

Grinding my teeth, I push the forearm with the dagger imbedded in it away from my chest, the fingers of my other hand fumbling to grip the sword that dropped from my hand when I hit the ground. I fling it in front of me just in time to stop the second dagger from cutting off my face. Using my legs, I kick the hunter off me, screaming when he takes both daggers with him and rips my skin open. Bright lights burst in front of me and my body moves more fluidly than ever before. Coiling my knees to my chest I kick out jumping to my feet.

The hunter crab-crawls away from whatever he sees on my face, but his end has come. I will enjoy taking his life for daring to bring this on top of our heads. He chose to be what he is. The fates made me what I am. It's time they understand the consequences of their foolish actions. My skin feels warm, liquid lapping at my face like the gentle waves of the ocean. It takes me long moments to hear someone calling my name.

"Francesca." Zoltan doesn't sound so commanding right now. "Look at me, Franky."

Hearing my nickname on his lips, I blink fast to bring his face into focus. He looks worried but I don't understand why. That's until his eyes flick to where I'm kneeling on the floor. I look down, noticing the sleek hold I have on the sword. A pile of limbs and body parts are rearranged like a grotesque painting at my feet. I swallow thickly, my mind going blank. I should be horrified, disgusted, or *something*.

I feel nothing.

The monstrosity who shares my body purrs in approval. They want to hurt us and everyone we are trying to protect. We will hurt them first, before that happens. No, not we. *I.* I will hurt them before they lay another finger on anyone I know. A ripple of energy passes through me from the bottom of my feet all the way to the crown of my head.

"Franky, look at me." Zoltan crouches behind the iron bars, bringing himself level with me. "You were protecting us. It's over now. Drop the sword and release me. It's okay." He gives me a reassuring nod and I tilt my head toward him. "Everything is going to be okay."

"Tha fios agam air, mo ghaol. A bheil thu eòlach air?" my voice purrs and Zoltan's eyes widen in shock.

Not having a clue what I just said, I shake my head slightly. Rising to my feet slowly, I keep my eyes on him. He does the same. With just one more glance at the mess at my feet, I turn and stride to the wall beside the stairs. I feel ready for something, but I have no idea what it is I'm ready for. Using the tip of the blood drenched sword, I flip the switch and the groan of metal sinking into concrete fills the room. Rotating to face Zoltan again, he stands completely still and doesn't stop looking at me.

I don't want to talk about what is going on with me or how I have no regrets of chopping the hunter into stew-sized pieces. Nor do I want to hear how everything is going to be alright. Because it won't. It'll never be alright again until Roberti is dealt with and these massacres stop once and for all. When the bars finally disappear inside the floor, I take a deep breath and release it slowly.

"Let's go." Spinning on my heel, I race up the stairs leaving Zoltan behind.

Chapter Seventeen

The hallway is more crowded than last time. Shifters, their animals reaching my chest in size, crawl and bounce off the walls while tearing hunters apart. I jump into the fight, slicing at anything dressed in white that comes my way. It's shocking how many people are here as back up. Surely nobody woke up this morning suspecting we'd be in the human world starting a war. I didn't have a clue, not until I got sucked into the portal beside Astara. For a fleeting moment, I hope she is okay.

A large panther shoulders me aside, a paw the size of my head swatting away a blade that is sailing right at my head. The shifter doesn't stop, instead pouncing on the closest hunter and ripping into his shoulder with a vicious snarl that makes me shiver. The hunters must be retreating towards the basement for this many people to crowd the hallway. The space is wide—wider than a typical house would be—but still narrow thanks to so many bodies everywhere. More than half of them are shifters, too, so they're a lot larger than their animal cousins would be.

Demons and mages pair up with each of them, keeping their back protected from flying daggers and deadly stars. If not for having to protect my own neck from being ripped open, I'd be staring in awe at how well they work together. Like a synchronized deadly dance, they twist and turn around each other, claws and jaws full of razor-sharp teeth seamlessly flowing with their muscled bodies. It's a pure example of what the academy is, of what it does for all the species. *Not what Roberti said,* the snide voice in my head reminds me.

I feel the heat coming at my back, my body reacting to Zoltan's nearness even when I kick and flip around to keep the hunters determined to slice me open away from me. His back bumps into mine and we fall into a familiar pattern. It's funny how he feels more like a partner, someone I trust to never let anything blindside me.

It feels nice.

The screams and roars of the hunters get louder when Zoltan takes his fury for being taken and turned feral out on them. Even the rest of the Daywalkers get more vicious, their attacks intensifying. It feels like seeing him among them removes any hesitancy on their part. I'm so focused on the change in their fighting I don't see a hunter getting closer until the glint of his blade catches my eye. I have no time to react, either, since my arms are too busy holding off two swords that will decapitate me if I lose focus.

The face of a snarling wolf with drool dripping from his open jaw sails in front of me and shoves me into Zoltan's back. The shifter clamps sharp teeth on the forearm of the hunter, ripping it off, the crunch of bone splitting the air. Blood splatters all over me and the wolf, the screams of the hunter cutting off when the shifter separates his head from the rest of the body. Another hunter jumps with daggers raised right at the wolf's back. My sword slices through the air decapitating the hunter, his body dropping at my feet while his head hits the wall over the wolf's head.

Leo shakes his fur, spraying me with more drops of blood.

"Good timing, mutt." I grin at his snarl.

"Good to see you, brother." Zoltan grunts as he punches a hunter in the face, caving his skull in.

Leo is right there ripping the throat out as the body falls to the ground. It's gruesome and I should feel appalled by the remorseful killing, but I'm not. My blood is thrumming through my veins with adrenaline while a purr of satisfaction vibrates my chest. Leo cocks his head to the side, his right ear flicking and turning my way at the sound. I pretend not to see it.

"Are we getting out of here or we are staying until we clean this place up." I fling to the side, taking Zoltan with me by yanking on his shoulder. The dagger hits the wall with a thump. "We need to find Astara and Fenrir."

Zoltan pulls me behind him, stepping right in my face. I blink at his back, but he already has a hunter by the neck and is lifting him off the ground. Using just his hands, he rips the body like it's made of paper and flings the two parts away from one another.

"They were at the foyer last time I saw them," Leo says, and I turn to him.

Standing in all his naked glory, hair mussed and muscles glinting from the sweat covering his skin, the asshole winks at me when my eyes drop to his erection. It juts out thick and proud like an arrow pointing a direction. I startle when a snarl is followed by my body being picked up and jerked behind Zoltan's back again.

Leo chuckles like he knows something I don't.

"Fighting makes the blood pump wherever it wants." The shifter laughs while Zoltan looms over him. "No offense, brother."

"Seriously, Zoltan." Shoving at his back doesn't move him an inch. "I can look if I feel like it."

"You will not." He doesn't even turn around as he grinds the words between clenched teeth.

"And who will stop me? You?" This is the most ridiculous conversation to have while we're in the middle of fighting for our lives. Even I can admit that.

"Yes." That one word sends a thrill through me.

"And this is my cue to get out of here." Leo chortles, the ass that he is. "I like keeping my dick attached to my body. I need it." From one blink to the next, he shifts back and lops down the hallway, his tail lashing the air.

I look around to search for someone to fight, but all I see both ways are empty halls, void of any and all signs of life. Just dead bodies litter the ground. My heart jumps to the back of my throat before plummeting to my feet.

Oh, shit.

I make it two steps from Zoltan before he grabs my arm and slams my back against the wall. His chest presses against me, freezing the breath in my lungs. My heart stops before it kicks into a frenzy in my chest. He is too close, breathing the same air as me. Instead of pushing him away, my body softens and molds into his like I'm fucking dough.

I knew I hated the stupid dress. Now when his hand grips my hip and the heat of his skin sinks into my bones, I know I've never loathed anything in my life as much as I do the silky fabric. My nipples turn into hard points, rasping against Zoltan's chest with each fast breath I take. His thumb rubbing small circles against my hipbone kicks up my arousal to unbearable levels and my thighs are slick while my channel pulses, clenching the emptiness there.

Zoltan bends his face closer to mine, pressing our foreheads together. My eyes close on their own as I breathe him in. He still smells like sin wrapped in skin, something forbidden but definitely irresistible. I guess this is how moths feel when they get too close to a flame. His sigh tightens my chest and I hold my breath. His thumb never stops moving in circles, sliding the silk over my skin and driving me insane. Even the hem of the dress where it's ripped feels tantalizing when it moves from the pull of his fingers.

"Thank you." I barely hear his voice from the thundering in my ears, but it vibrates from his chest into mine.

"Bad timing buddy, our friends are fighting for their lives out there." It's really embarrassing how breathless I sound. Each word catches on my heart thumping in my throat, but I don't move away.

He presses me further into the wall like he is trying to turn our bodies into one being. I'm trying very hard—trying and failing miserably—to ignore the hard erection poking my belly. It's like a brand short-circuiting my brain. Oh, who am I kidding? That's all I'm aware of right now. Roberti can be standing with a dagger at my throat and I still won't be able to get my head out of the gutter. I want him like never before. Maybe seeing him feral and coming close to my own end killed some braincells and turned me into the horny, quivering mess standing in front of him now.

He is a pure blood, Franky. Don't be stupid. Even that voice in my head sounds too distant to have an effect.

"I should've known you'd come for me." Zoltan is dealing with his own demons, I realize. "I wanted you as far from them as possible, but I should've known ..." Another sigh is dragged from his chest.

"Roberti kinda made it personal. Don't think too highly of yourself." The vampire does not need more fuel for his arrogance.

"You came for me." There is not even a sliver of doubt in his voice.

"The academy needs you." There, that sounds reasonable, right?

Pulling back slightly, his other hand grips the back of my neck. His damn thumb is still moving, and thanks to the thin fabric, he has surely already seen the reaction he has on me. Unless he's blind, which he isn't. His nostrils flare and I wish for a hunter to come out of nowhere and save me from my misery. He can smell my reaction as much as he can see it. *Way to go Franky. Way to fuckin' go.*

Caught in his gaze like a deer in headlights, I stare back at him, my mouth drying up. I refuse to acknowledge the emotions playing in the blue depths. Master of denial, I wet my dry lips and he locks all his attention on the movement of my tongue. A deep growl sends another wave of arousal through me. I'm soaking wet and the dress will soon show how pathetic I am. Trying to press my thighs together to elevate the need, I squirm restlessly before freezing.

My idiotic movement slides his thigh between my legs, and he takes advantage of it without missing a beat. He hasn't looked away from my face, cataloging every flutter or my lashes, every hitch of my breath, and the dilation of my pupils. I have no doubt that I have a glazed look in my eyes. Even my head is full of mush as my need for him thrums through it. His gaze flicks to the pulse beating erratically in my neck and his lids drop to half-mast. All I hear is myself screaming inside my head. *oh fuck, fuck, fuck … fuck. This is so not happening here.*

"But you never do what I tell you to do, isn't that right?" There is a raw edge to his voice that turns my insides into lava. "You love breaking the rules."

"You break the rules too," I point out just for the sake of saying something.

"True." His lips lift at the corners to show just the glimpse of the tips of his fangs under them.

I whimper.

His thigh is moving just enough to make me crazy, and it's preventing me from being able to think. I don't even know I'm breathing until I take a few pathetic gasps. Wanting Zoltan from afar, or even flirting with him—and let's not forget dry humping him like an idiot—is one thing. Sex with any male can be whatever you want to call it, a quick fuck, a hump in the dark, or a mistake. Or ignore it as a lack of judgment on your part. The vampire looking at me like he wants to drink in my soul and bind me to him for eternity is not one of those males. He will screw me up for the rest of my life and hurt me. I've stayed away from developing any form of closeness with everyone in my life, including my own parents, for that very reason.

I am a half blood.

No matter how much they need me, none will ever need Francesca Drake. They need my blood, or bloodline as Fenrir pointed out. How much of this is Zoltan seeing and wanting Francesca, and how much is a powerful Daywalker scoring a power point in the war we started? Those thoughts bring my libido down a bit, clearing the fog in my head. My lips part so I can tell him to let me go.

The world tilts around me when Zoltan swings me over his shoulder. My head is dangling above the round globes of his ass while I watch his powerful thighs eat up the space from the wall to the door of the basement. I don't have time to voice my outrage before he spins again, slamming the door closed and pushing my back against it.

I feel the touch of his lips on mine and my brain turns off.

Chapter Eighteen

I expect him to be rough, dominant, and downright harsh in the way he kisses me. My shoulders stiffen when he takes his time, devouring my mouth like some gourmet cuisine he wants to savor. Angling my face the way he wants it, his tongue swirls around mine in sensual, slow strokes before he sucks it gently into his mouth. My entire being comes to life, and I claw on his shoulders to bring him closer. Or maybe it's to push him away. I'm not sure what I want in this moment. I think Zoltan is one of those people that enjoy kissing as an integral part of intimacy. And he has had a very long time to perfect his skill. Enough to make me forgo breathing just so I don't ever have to remove my lips from his.

I knew he would destroy me for eternity.

I just didn't know it'd be with a kiss.

Pulling back, he nips on my bottom lip before gliding his tongue over the sting. Slow kisses are peppered over my face until he gently presses his mouth on the corner of my lips, flicking his tongue there just for a split second. Then he surprises me by nuzzling his face to mine, the skin of our cheeks grazing. Taking a deep breath, he leans his forehead on my shoulder, still keeping me pinned to the door as both of his arms tighten around me.

I would've preferred it if he fucked me stupid and left me to pick up the pieces.

Males like Zoltan don't show weakness.

It takes me a second to blink away the daze and unclench my fingers that are digging into his shoulders. Closing my eyes, I tentatively reach my hand and spear my fingers through his hair. His deep sigh breaks my heart and I press my cheek to the side of his head. Zoltan crushes me harder to his chest when I wrap my other arm around his shoulders. We stand like that for a while, neither my libido nor his erection taking the hint and going away.

"I could've killed you." The bones of my ribcage protest in his punishing grip.

"You didn't." The spike in my heartbeat doesn't go unnoticed. I'm not sure if I'm trying to convince him that everything is fine, or myself.

"I was aware deep inside that it was you." His deep voice drums through both of us. "I was raging inside my mind to stop but I couldn't do anything about it." He nips my shoulder in punishment. "What were you thinking?"

"I didn't let you loose. Myst did." I bite my tongue hard. Why the hell did I bring that psycho up?

"I'll have a word with her about it." My blood curdles at the threat in his words.

"She did save you from your feral state, and me from a certain death." I keep running my fingers through his matted hair because I can't help myself. "I don't think she wanted us dead. She just needs to finetune her tactics."

"Sounds like someone else I know," Zoltan drawls, and I thump my knuckles over his skull.

He growls.

"There is a method to my madness, I'll have you know." Chuckling weakly, I breathe through my nose in hopes my body will get the hint we are not having sex because when the male before me makes those sounds, it's not getting the memo.

"I'm looking forward to figuring it out." His face turns and he drags his lips to the hollow where my neck meets my shoulder. "And I'm going to take my time learning everything you are, Francesca Drake." His lips graze my skin with each word he speaks, making me shiver involuntarily.

"We should go meet the others," I choke out when he starts kissing a slow path towards my ear.

"Mmmm." His chest vibrates. "We should." His tongue swirls out and takes the earring dangling from my lobe in his mouth, tugging on it.

"We should," I repeat as I struggle to breathe.

"They'll be fine for just a few more moments." His hand burns a path from my back around my hip until I feel his fingers curling under the hem of the ripped dress.

I shouldn't have ripped it.

The silk tickles my thighs as he painfully and ever-so-slowly tugs it up, the tips of his fingers pebbling my skin. He sweeps the edge of my panties, up and down, back and forth. I can't stop the low moan that comes from deep in my throat. Zoltan groans at the sound, then his fingers slip inside. His thigh nudges my legs apart and he dips between the folds of my wet center.

Back arching, my knees go weak and I sag against him. He presses his chest harder on mine, crushing my breasts so hard my nipples poke him. It sends a delicious thrill through my insides. Zoltan takes his time, the rough pads of his fingers gliding through my nether lips with controlled strokes. Circling my entrance makes me moan again. My hand tightens in his hair. Without giving me reprieve, he plunges two fingers inside me, his thumb pressing hard on my nub.

"First, I need you to fall apart in my hands, Francesca." He kisses the daylights out of me, my eyes rolling to the back of my head. "I almost lost you, so I need to feel you alive."

I chase his lips when he moves away with a whimper of protest and he chuckles with arrogant male pride at the power he has over me. The pumping of his fingers doesn't ease, and I feel the tightening in my lower belly getting to the point of no return. My hips move in pursuit of his hand and the release it promises. The tempo of his hand is fast and unyielding, but his kiss stays the same, a seductive dance of our tongues. I think I'll go insane if he moves away.

Releasing my grip on his hair, I shove my hand between us and fumble with the button of his pants. He pulls his hips away to give me room to yank them open and wrap my fingers around the hard, warm flesh of his shaft. Zoltan grunts in pleasure and starts swiveling his hips, gliding his erection in my hand at the same time as his fingers stretch my channel. Our breathing speeds up and his kisses become less controlled, more frantic. It gives me an adrenaline surge to see him lose control. I tighten my hand on his cock and he grabs a handful of my hair, jerking my head to the side. I clench around his fingers, sucking them in just as his fangs sink into the skin of my neck.

The orgasm hits me like a tsunami. My body jerks and twists in his arms, and I taste my own blood from biting my lip to stop myself from screaming his name. He pumps his hips faster, his cock swelling in my fingers while he drags deep mouthfuls of my blood, animalistic growls rumbling from his chest. Fingers still pumping inside me, he pulls his fangs away but swirls his tongue over the punctures before he erupts in my hand.

"Francesca." My name is a deep groan passing his lips before his mouth crushes mine, the warmth spurting from his cock all over my hand and wrist.

We stand like that for several moments, both of us breathing heavily and Zoltan's fingers still inside me, his hand cupping between my thighs possessively. I'm still not satisfied. I'm not sure I'll ever have enough until he is inside me, and I have a weird feeling not even then. He is too addictive for my own good, but like the moth and all that, I guess I never learn a lesson the easy way. He is still gyrating his hips, pumping in my hand lazily as if he doesn't want the moment to end. Judging by how hard he still is, I have no doubt we can stay here for a few hours more, if not longer.

With great reluctance he moves away, holding my upper arms until I nod that I'm good to stand on my own two feet. Tucking himself in, he jumps down the stairs in two long loops. I frown and wonder what he is doing until I see him ripping the shirt of the hunter with the broken neck at the bottom of the stairs. The dead bodies in this room don't even enter my mind while having Zoltan's all-consuming presence wrapped around me like my own personal bubble.

Taking the stairs three at a time, he comes back. Taking my hand, he cleans it up with an unnerving focus. His grip is gentle as he turns my wrist this way and that. When he deems it fit, he lifts it to his face and presses a soft kiss to the center of my palm. I swallow thickly, keeping my mouth shut so I don't say something stupid. Zoltan rubs the balled-up fabric over the mess on his shredded clothing and on my dress. We are both covered in varying degrees of drying blood, so the evidence of our lust is hardly noticeable.

The scent of it clinging to our skin is a totally different matter.

You should've thought of that before riding his fingers, Franky. I shove that stupid voice as far in the back of my head as I can.

Chucking the dirty shirt aside, Zoltan looks around before facing me. I know my face is turning red, but I refuse to look away from him. When his look softens at my tilted chin I want to scream. I don't, but I really, really want to. Cupping my face in his large hand, he rubs his thumb over my cheekbone.

"We have a lot to talk about, mo ghaol." My stomach does a freefall somersault when he kisses my forehead. "First, let's see what's going on out there."

He pulls me to the side and opens the door, sticking his head out to check if anyone is waiting for us. I follow him dumbly, still shocked at how nice and natural it felt for him to be gentle—almost loving—like that with me. It's a very dangerous way of thinking on my part but I can't help it. I'll blame it on hormones and post orgasmic bliss later on, I'm sure.

Tugging on my hand, Zoltan leads me out of the basement and down the hall. I move faster to compensate for his longer strides, that way he doesn't have to drag me behind him like a child. Then it hits me what he said.

"What did I say to you back when you were playing a monkey in a cage?" Okay, so I could've phrased it better, but he has enough shit to stroke his ego. I need to bring him down a notch … or ten.

"You don't know?" He looks at me over his shoulder, but I'm pretending to pay attention to where we're going.

"Not all of us speak hundreds of languages and we haven't all had centuries to learn them, either."

"You spoke it, not me." I really want to slap the amusement off his face.

"Yeah, well you have Fenrir to thank for that." Glaring at him, I raise my chin. "He made this monster inside of me blend in and speak. I had nothing to do with it, nor can I control what it says."

In the back of my mind an idea forms. I can blame my dragon blood for acting deprived and getting all hot and heavy with Zoltan while dead bodies witnesses our little hump. My eyes flick to his face and the idea dies a sudden death from the knowing look he gives me. Grinding my teeth, I dismiss it. Fine, I'll own up to being a horny freak. Damn vampires and their mind fucks.

"He did well if he helped you integrate your magic. I remember Soren at the beginning having the same problem." My eyebrows crawl up my forehead and hide in my hairline. Zoltan chuckles. "He told me about it, but I wasn't around to witness it. I'm not that old."

"You're still a cradle robber, mister."

Throwing his head back, he laughs.

I stare at his throat working and the softening of the lines on his face. My lips twitch despite my trying to stay pissed at him. Then he squeezes my fingers, which he's holding in his hand, and tugs on my arm good-naturedly. My insides turn to mush and, as stupid as I am, I'm surprised I don't melt into a puddle on the floor.

"You said, 'I know that my love.' Did you know?" It takes me a moment to understand that he translated my dual personality glitch.

"I did not call you *my* anything. Stop making shit up." I try to jerk my hand away as we round a corner, but of course he doesn't allow it.

"You'll call me many things of yours when we get home." I have to swallow the lump in my throat at his heated gaze.

Home. What a strange way to phrase his or Fenrir's apartment. I almost slap my forehead when it dawns on me that he is talking about the academy. As much as I like to talk crap just to naysay him, he has a very good point. Somewhere along the way, Daywalker Academy became my home. Warmth spreads through my chest at that.

It disappears just as fast.

"I have a problem with you going anywhere." Alexius stands at the entrance of the foyer where the long hallway ends, his arms folded across his chest.

Chapter Nineteen

"Alexius." Zoltan's voice is harsh, and I feel like running the other way just hearing it. I'm not sure how Alexius stays facing him.

I bristle when he nudges me behind him, the protective shit getting too frustrating to ignore. Not wanting to encourage any remarks from Alex, I grind my teeth but still step out to position myself next to the arrogant male. His shoulders stiffen slightly but thankfully he keeps his mouth shut. The two males are glaring at each other, so I have the time to look over Alex's shoulder into the large, open area behind him.

While we were secluded in our basement, everyone has continued to fight. There are too many people crowded together. They look like a shifting sea of black and white as they move around each other. A line of hunters is standing guard behind Alexius, protecting him from any of our people stabbing his stupid ass. Quite unfortunate, if you ask me.

"Zoltan, I see you've had a little snack." Cocking his

head to the side, Alex narrows his eyes and glances from me to Zoltan. "I wondered if her blood could cure the poisoning from the potion." I almost miss the muttering under his breath. "I'm happy to have my assumptions confirmed." Speaking louder, he seems like he is growing in size when his arms drop to his sides. "Unfortunately, it means I can't allow you to take her out of here."

"It's a good thing I'm not asking for permission."

"You can try to stop me." I speak at the same time as Zoltan.

A muscle ticks in Alex's jaw, at the same time as one jumps in Zoltan's. What can I say? I'm a woman of many talents. Pissing arrogant males off seems to be my specialty. A grin spreads across my face the longer Alex glowers at me. If the jerk expects me to let Zoltan fight my battles, he will be sorely disappointed. I may be a fish out of water when navigating the human world and dealing with daylight, but I'm way too familiar with putting assholes in their place. I've done it my whole life.

"Oh, this asshole is mine." Anger sparks up inside me when the hunter Zoltan called Jack steps next to Alexius. "Don't you dare touch him; his ugly mug has a lot to answer for," I hiss at Zoltan before he dares to shove me behind him again.

"Arrogance can get you killed fast, Drake," he growls under his nose and I turn to look at him incredulously.

"You don't say." Sandpaper has nothing on the dryness of my words.

Zoltan grins at me. There is no humor in the tilt of his lips.

"Stay safe, Drake." My pulse leaps at the intent look in his eyes. "I'll kill you myself if you get hurt."

Facing Alex and the hunter, I roll my shoulders. "Ditto,

buddy." My stomach clenches when he chuckles next to me. "I'll keep your feral ass for entertaining the masses on a daily basis if you let them poison you again."

"I have plans for you as soon as we get out of here, Francesca." Both of us bend our knees when the two males move toward us. "Nothing will stand in the way of finishing what we started, that I promise you." Well, as for motivation goes, I must admit the vampire has it down pat.

Kill the assholes now, have sex later.

It works for me.

Alexius and the hunter move cautiously towards us, their eyes darting to judge when we will move. Planning attacks has never worked for me so far, so I do what I've always done best. Jumping up, I bounce with one foot off Zoltan's thigh and sail through the air right at Jack. He is still far enough away that I use the wall to propel my body further, taking advantage of the momentum to force Alexius a couple of steps back so they don't end up on the ground together.

Jack hunches in preparation of our collusion but the idiot doesn't know I have something else in mind. I feel Zoltan right at my heels, his feet thumping on the ground while I move on the sides of the wall like gravity has no pull on my weight. The world bursts into colors and the hunter's eyes bulge out like they're ready to pop out of their sockets. He tightens his grip on the daggers in his hands, but I don't give him time to even lift his arms and use his weapons.

My fangs drop from my gums and I tear into the closest forearm, shaking my head and ripping out a chuck of muscle just as my shoulder hits him full force in the chest. We crash into the wall on the side, the daggers clinking on the ground when they slip from his fingers. There is a loud slap of two bodies smacking into each other when Alex and

Zoltan slam together. It's disappointing that the hunter doesn't make a sound even when his nasty blood fills my mouth.

I'm spitting it out and trying not to gag when he shoves me away from him. My ribs protest when I hit the opposite wall hard, barely missing the slashing claws from the two vampires fighting without holding back. Jack is up too fast, facing me with one arm bleeding like an open faucet at his feet. The stench of the tainted fluid is overwhelming to my senses so I breathe through my mouth. It doesn't seem to bother anyone else.

Not waiting on the hunter to make up his mind, I throw myself at him again. He grabs my raised knee that is going for his chest, but my forehead connects to his nose. The injured arm is slowing him down just enough to allow me to pummel him with fast jabs on the side of his ribs. His white clothing was dirty before but now it's turning into a nice shade of dark red from being drenched in his blood. I don't stop punching, the muscles of my arms burning from the speed of my movements. If I pause for a second, I'll lose my advantage and I have no intention of doing that.

Bones crack and crunch under my knuckles while he grapples at my body in a futile attempt to stop the assault. Rage at what he did to me, to Astara the first time I encountered the hunters, is turning my vision red. All sound of fighting fades away and my entire being is centered on the creature I want gone from this world. Power pulses in my chest with its own heartbeat and sends a jolt of excitement through my limbs. I smile for a moment, feeling wonderful that he will die right here. The curl of my lips is wiped clean when I'm thrown away from him with such force my head hits something unforgiving, a loud crack echoing through the space around us.

Dark spots dance in front of my eyes for a second as I blink slowly, completely dazed from the impact. What the hell happened? There is no way the hunter has any strength left in him to throw me like that. Familiar skin touches mine when a hand grabs my upper arm and yanks me to my feet. Zoltan is right next to me snarling like a beast at something in front of us. It takes another long moment for the world to stop spinning so I can see what he sees.

I almost swallow my tongue.

The hunter is standing on his feet, his entire body and face caved in from my pummeling while blood drips freely from everywhere. A dark, thick shadow is extended from his body, writhing like a million serpents snapping at us. The most terrifying face stretches out of his features, the empty eyes of the incorporeal being stabbing me in the center of the chest. It's no longer Zoltan holding me upright. My nails dig into his skin, gripping him for dear life. Even the magic inside me shrinks at the unknown monster staring at us.

"I don't fucking think so." A female voice cheers from my right and a blast of horrible-smelling liquid splashes the hunter, soaking him up from head to toe. The shadows blink out of existence with a teeth-jarring screech.

Jack drops on the ground like a puppet with his strings cut off.

My head jerks to the side and I gape at Myst. The female is grinning proudly, a large white bucket dangling from her hand. I stare frozen until she winks at me, her nostrils flaring. Alex, who is as stupefied as Zoltan and me, gets animated in that moment. Myst swings the bucket and smacks him across his face. Before he takes even two steps, he staggers back with one hand clutching his broken nose.

With a snarl, Alexius turns his attention to her. With my

eyes so focused on Myst, I don't miss the hurt that crosses her face. It is there for a second and gone the next, so I almost think I imagine it when she cocks her hip and curls the fingers on her hand in an invitation. That crazed look is back in her eyes and the smile looks like it never left her pretty face. Zoltan moves to intercept Alex.

"I got this, hot stuff," Myst drawls at Zoltan, stopping both him and Alexius in their tracks. "Me and him have some unresolved issues to settle." Twisting his lip in disgust at her words, Alex takes a step toward her. "I don't think a quickie was enough for your girl there. Take her home. I've got this."

Because the situation is what it is, I don't even feel mortified that she smells the lingering scent of sex on me. As it is, I'm just standing here expecting Zoltan to ignore her and rip Alex a new one. Color me surprised when he simply nods at her, respect blanketing his features before he turns to me. I frown at the dumbass. He can't possibly leave the petite female—no matter how crazy she is or the fact that she set me up to almost die—to deal with the vampire that looks like he can break her in half with one hand tied behind his back.

Neither me telling Zoltan off nor Myst fighting a losing battle comes to pass. It's like that shriek from the shadow was an alarm going off, and all the remaining hunters go into a frenzy. They start fighting with desperation that makes them uncoordinated but more deadly by far. It's like they have nothing to lose at this point so they throw themselves on claws and blades with no care for their lives.

The hallway is swarmed with fighting bodies separating me and Zoltan from Myst and the female from Alexius. I lose sight of her when I must move so I don't end up skewered on the edge of a dagger or a sword. Falling back into the rhythm of fighting alongside Zoltan, all I look for is white clothing so I can rip into the person wearing it.

At some point we step out of the narrow passage and into the foyer, which is more open and allows easier movement even though it turns us into bigger targets. I manage to take a look around, and I'm shocked anew at how many people Fenrir and Leo brought with them. It's like three quarters of the academy is here fighting with the intent focus of killing everything in sight. Too bad I don't catch a glimpse of Roberti. That coward must've fled the first change he got. Ever since I've known him, he intimidated all of Sienna by getting the rest of us do his dirty work. Just his name was used to bring fear. Funny how things become clear when you get sucker punched by betrayal and you can finally see clearly.

The air around us thins out as more hunters drop lifelessly on the floor. The stench of sweat, blood, and death sinks into every pore of my skin. I doubt I'll be able to wash it off for months. Fur brushes against my bare thighs and I see Leo has come next to us, pouncing on any hunter stupid enough, or alive enough, to comes near us. When one of the suckers drops in front of me, I get a clear view on Myst being herded to a corner by two hunters. She looks like a deadly doll, moving with grace and each kick or punch she throws out landing with staggering accuracy. Platinum hair catches my attention closer to her than anyone else. Fenrir is flinging hunters off him like a battering ram, hair flying around his perfect face and making him look like an avenging angel. Deadly perfection is the only way to describe what I'm seeing.

"Fenrir!" yelling out his name, I kick a hunter away from me before locking my eyes on his. "Help her!" I wince when a blade slashes too close to her neck.

The blood turns into icicles in my veins when Fenrir turns to look at Myst and simply ignores the female. Giving her his back, he continues moving in our direction with renewed strength. If I don't know better, I may say he is trying his best to get as far away from her as he can. The Fae can be annoying and arrogant with the best of them. Even cruel and menacing, as I witnessed when he was dealing with the mage who came to heal me and Astara. I never think to see him as heartless, but the way he glances at her dispassionately is the only thing I can call it. Heartless and almost as if he wants her dead.

What the hell is wrong with him?

"Leo, you need to help Myst." Even Zoltan cranes his neck when I huff at the shifter. "They have her cornered and more are making their way to her."

The wolf snarls while barreling through everything standing in his way. Shouts of surprise or anger follow him as he disappears through the bodies. I finally breathe easier when I see Astara, alive and well albeit with blood all over her, stepping next to Myst. The female has help and that leaves me to deal with mine. I ignore Fenrir when he finally steps next to us. Between the three of us, we reach the center of the foyer much faster than expected, coming face to face with Astara and Myst. All the people from the academy are looking around in case someone still lingering is alive. Dead hunters cover the floor at our feet like a grotesque rug. And then the weirdest thing in this messed up night happens.

Every single person turns their attention to me.

One by one, as my gaze connects to theirs, demons, shifters and mages nod their heads and murmur, "Drake."

Goosebumps pop up along my skin, and I squirm uncomfortably under the weight of their intent stares. My heart slows down when the heat from Zoltan's hand on my lower back stops my panic. What is going on? Why are they looking at me like they are seeing me for the first time? It can't be the damn sex smell still clinging to my skin. The stench of death is too strong even for their sensitive noses.

"How did you get all these people to come on such short notice, Fae?" As much as I don't feel like talking to him, I can't help but ask.

"They are not here because we called them for back up." Fenrir's voice has a tone of wonder in it, and that confuses the shit out of me.

"What do you mean?" I press my back closer to Zoltan's hand, the only thing stopping me from bolting out of here.

"They came to back you up, Hellion," Fenrir murmurs, a note of pride ringing from his words. "The moment Leo mentioned your name, every single one of them ran through the portal. They followed you, not us."

Chapter Twenty

"Okay, so they all came for Zoltan." The knot forming in my stomach loosens at that.

"Actually"—Leo steps closer again in his birthday suit, and for a minute I don't even notice him joining us— "I only had time to say Alexius has Francesca. They swarmed out of the academy, spreading the word as they went."

"Yes, because they knew I was going after Zoltan." I cling to that like pushing a pull door. They have no idea what they're talking about.

"I actually very much doubt they are here because of my brother." Astara steps to Zoltan's other side and he tucks her under his arm. "Not in these numbers anyway."

I look around the faces again, aware those closest to us can hear our conversation. That knot that loosened is now tying my insides, twisting like a fist inside me. They must be wrong. I'm a loner and I like it that way. Having the four of them—as much as I'm angry at Fenrir at the moment—is more than I've ever allowed myself. As the only other friend

I've had, Daren would say I'm too prickly for anyone to want to get close to me. Again, just how I like it.

"They have no reason to be here just to watch my back." Hissing at the Fae, I clench my fists because I don't want to snap at Astara for encouraging this stupid idea.

"You chose us." It's not Fenrir or any of my friends answering my outburst. "They stood there holding the one you'd willingly die to protect with a knife under his throat and you chose to protect us."

I blink at the mage standing in front of me with his shoulders pulled back.

"Between your heart and the rest of us, you picked Sienna when they threatened to bring down the portals," a demon I've never seen before grumbles from behind the mage. More of them crowd closer around us. "We can fight to protect ourselves, but all of us have families that will be slaughtered if the hunters have free access to everyone. That type of loyalty cannot be bought or forced into any of us." The demon squirms uncomfortably at the same time I do. You can hear a pin drop. "You have no reason to trust my kind when many have turned traitors and worked against you, yet you fought alongside us and had our back. We will pay you back in kind until our last breath, Drake." Thumping his chest, he spins on his heels and walks away.

I find it difficult to breathe.

"That was Crim; he leads the demons in the academy. Like Leo is the alpha of the shifters," Zoltan whispers in my ear, his breath tinkling my skin.

"I don't want this." Wiping my sweaty palms on my thighs, I swallow the lump the size of a tennis ball that's trying to choke me. Not even the vampire's hand rubbing my back is helping right now.

"You see us as equal to you and each other. The mages

and Fae will follow your lead and have your back until our last breath as well." The mage thumps his chest as well.

Zoltan leans toward me again.

"If you say a word, I'm going to scratch your eyes out." I elbow him to keep him away.

He grunts but still chuckles.

Asshole.

"I don't have to tell you the same goes for the shifters, Drake," Leo says, casually stretching his arms over his head. "We've waited a long time for something like this. You have our loyalty, no questions asked."

I'm very proud of myself for keeping my eyes on his face. That's until Zoltan chuckles again when my heartbeat triples from Leo's words. Shifting so he has a perfect view of my face, I pointedly lock my gaze on the shifter's cock, which is still an acting arrow. The shaft jerks and jumps slightly at my scrutiny. Leo's grin matches mine when Zoltan snarls. Shaking his head, the shifter leaves, hopefully looking for some pants.

"This is so screwed up." I rub a hand over my face my mouth, twisting in disgust when flakes of dry blood crumble from it. "I'm a walking disaster waiting to happen. I know it, you know it, and everyone that's ever heard of me knows it too. They'll follow me right off the cliff soon enough."

"You'll be fine, Hellion." Fenrir touches my shoulder but I flinch away from him. "They needed hope. You instigated a new order simply by being yourself. It's not a bad thing." If me cringing away hurts him, he doesn't show it. "You know the three of us will always have your back no matter what."

"Like you had Myst's back?" The words are out before I can stop them.

My eyes flick around scanning the wide space for the

female. Fenrir stays silent, at least not making excuses for his shitty behavior. I see Myst sitting alone as far from everyone as possible, leaning on the wall with her forearms resting on her bent knees. Her eyes are closed, but the moment my gaze finds her they open and lock on me. It's unnerving how she knows the second I notice where she is. Her blood is still in my veins and it feels familiar and terrifying at the same time. Now that the adrenaline is gone, I am tired to the marrows of my bones. That makes it easier to analyze what her blood does to me. As stupid as it sounds, I think it made me stronger and more immune to the hits I took. How is that possible?

Zoltan follows my gaze, so when I step away from him he doesn't yank me back. I hear him talking to his sister in hushed tones as I weave my way through dead bodies and people sitting among them just to catch their breath. Good thing this place is away from humans because no amount of illusion can hide us from them. Not with the war zone in this place. Funny enough, I don't see Roberti or Alexius dead on the floor.

"You did well, Chicca," Myst says as I slide down the wall to sit next to her. I keep my legs stretched in front of me so my ass—or any other parts for that matter—doesn't show.

"I'm glad you are not hurt." Feeling awkward, I blurt it out to make up for Fenrir's assholiness. "It was amazing to see you fight."

"That's like telling someone it's amazing to see them breathe, Chicca." She smiles to take away the snark. "Fighting is all I know. It comes in handy in situations like this."

"I can say the same." She gives me a strange look, but I keep my face straight while looking around at everyone.

"Thank you for helping with …" my voice trails off before I add, "everything" lamely.

"Don't sound too grateful or you'll make me cry." Snickering, she bumps her shoulder on mine.

I smile despite everything, but it fades quickly. "Alexius got away, huh?"

"It's what cowards like him do." Shrugging a shoulder, she picks at the dried blood smeared over her forearms. "When they realize they are outnumbered, they flee. I'll find him soon enough, don't you worry."

"Just like Roberti," I muse, watching as if fascinated how she flakes the blood off her skin.

"Mhm," she hums absently before giving me the full impact of her knowing gaze. "Being the center of attention doesn't sit well with you."

It's not a question so I don't answer, just shrug one shoulder like I'm not bothered by it.

"They desperately needed a change in that place if you ask me." She gets all my focus with that statement. "Calling themselves Daywalkers like they are the same while separating everyone into a pyramid of casts was bound to bite them in the ass." We sit silent for a long time, and when I think that's all she'll say she speaks again. "It was not always like that from what I've been told."

"From Alexius?" Her jaw clenches for a second at my question.

"I woke up at the academy doors one day." Luckily, she doesn't leave me confused for long. "I don't remember how I got there, or anything else in my life before that day."

"You are a Daywalker?" I frown when she smiles but it doesn't reach her eyes.

"No, I stayed there just a couple of months before

coming to the human realm." I stop her fingers from scratching the skin on her arms raw. "I never looked back."

"Is that why Fenrir has his knickers stuck up his ass?" I bite on my tongue. What's wrong with me prying into people's personal lives even though I don't want them doing the same?

"No." Myst chuckles but I don't miss the sadness hidden behind it. "We have a bit of history together. And before your imagination takes off, no there was no hunky dories happening and no wild monkey sex either. "

"Okay."

"He is not my type," she adds when I keep my questions to myself, confirming that the Fae is very much her type. I know because that's exactly what I say about Zoltan.

As if reading my mind, I can feel his eyes on me, but I force myself not to look his way.

"I get it." The vampire turns me inside out from across the room, damn him. "No one likes that perfect face or killer body, right? It'll give any female a complex."

"Right," Myst agrees a bit too fast.

"So, what's your plan after tonight?" An idea swirls in my head as I give Myst a side-eyed glance. "You plan on going after Alexius on your own?"

"I've been hunting down morons on my own since I can remember." She looks up and I know Zoltan is making his way toward us without seeing him. "I work best alone."

"You can come with us for a day or two. Even a Tasmanian devil like yourself needs a break from time to time." We both giggle at the comparison.

"Thank you, but no." She climbs to her feet, and I follow groaning when my legs protest at the movement. "Too many people give me a headache. I need my isolation time to recover, not someone constantly breathing down my neck."

The way her eyes find Fenrir when she says it tells me there is more to the story than just chemistry between them. No matter how much the Fae kicks like a stubborn donkey, I know he is not indifferent when it comes to Myst just by his drastic reactions to her. I'm very tempted to ask her what she knows about the book Alexius tried to steal but something holds me back. Zoltan being almost next to us is not helping either.

"How do I get in touch with you if I need you?" She's already turning away but my question stops her.

"You have an academy full of competent fighters ready to go through fire with you. Why would you need me?" She is watching me over her shoulder, her face tilted slightly up.

"I don't know." I'm acting indifferent but I have a nagging feeling there will be a day that I'll need her more than anyone else. My pulse spikes up at that thought. "You never know," I tell her. "Maybe I'll need you or you'll need me. It's good to have a way to get in touch if that's the case. You know you can find me at the academy. I have no choice but to be there."

"Leave this at any portal you exit if you ever need me." After watching me for a long time she speaks, sticking her hand at me. I open my palm and she drops a small rock in it. It looks like a piece of coal. "I'll come no later than an hour from the time you drop it on the ground, a lot faster if I'm close by. Unless I'm dead."

My heart skips a beat at how nonchalant she sounds about dying.

"Thank you." It sounds inadequate but it's all I can think of. "What are you Myst?" My curiosity about the female cannot be stopped. "I'm usually very good at figuring people out, but not you."

Her mouth opens but her eyes flick over my shoulder and her entire demeanor changes into the cocky attitude I associate with her. Zoltan steps next to me, his hand going to my lower back at the same time. It's a possessive move that should irk me. It turns my knees weak instead.

"A Fae." She grins at both of us before walking away. "Couldn't you tell? We are very much alike."

She doesn't look at me for that last part, nor does she stop moving away. I'm sure she means it as reassuring, or maybe it's her way of being evasive just to shut me up. She doesn't count on the monstrosity in my chest perking up at her words and paying very close attention. Myst may have told the truth about being a Fae. Everything in me tells me it's actually very important to know just exactly what type of Fae she is. Right now, not knowing seems pretty harmless.

I have a feeling it'll be very important soon enough, though.

Chapter Twenty-One

My head is resting on the cool glass of the window while the vehicle zooms through the streets of the human world. The rocking of it lulls me into a daze where I stare unseeing at the colors and lights blurring around me. Everything hurts. Now that I don't have to move or fight to stay alive, I feel tired to the bone. Can your hair hurt? I think mine is smarting pretty good right now.

"You doing okay there, Franky?" Astara leans over me, getting in my face.

"Yeah." Sighing, I lean back on the seat and roll my head to the side so I can look at her. "Just zoning out I think."

"You did good tonight, girl." Her eyes glitter when light from the passing city hits it through the window. "We did more damage to the hunters than we've been able to do in years. It'll take them a while to recover from it."

"Alexius and Roberti got away." The dead bodies littering the mansion push to the front of my mind, but I shake the vision away. "I didn't see Cassius either. I'm glad they blew the place up though. Too bad those idiots weren't inside when it happened."

"Still bloodthirsty?" Fenrir looks over his shoulder from the passenger seat.

Searching his face, I say nothing, and his smile turns into a thin press of his lips. I still can't get over the fact that he just walked away from Myst while she was being cornered. No male should leave a female to fend for herself. Unless she's the enemy, which the more I think about her actions the more I very much doubt. Crazy? She is absolutely insane. Evil? I don't think so.

Blue eyes bore into my face from the rearview mirror. Zoltan is driving and has the steering wheel gripped tight in his large hands, but instead of watching the road he is staring at me. My stomach backflips at that intent look, so I duck to the side and use his seat as a cover. Yeah, I'm a coward. I know.

"What was in that bucket that Myst threw at the hunter?" That's been nagging at me since it happened. It's good for a change of subject, as well. "It had a strong scent of salt in it." My nose wrinkles at the thought. Even through the stench of blood and gore, the salt seared my nostrils.

"Saltwater." Astara giggles like it's a known joke. I lift my eyebrow at her. "Just that, honestly. Salt repels evil spirits and demonic entities. It was a very quick thinking on her part." Grinning brightly, she nods her head at something that only she apparently knows. "That female is always prepared, I'll tell ya. For as long as I've known her, I've yet to see anyone get one over on her. She's as slippery as a snake."

Fenrir stiffens in the passenger seat, so I let the subject drop.

My fingers rub over the small piece of coal Myst gave me, the lump scraping over the pad of my thumb. Gnawing on the inside of my cheek, I can't help but roll the possibilities through my head. No matter how pissed she was at Alexius, Myst had no need to go out of her way to help us. She could've shared info, or even come along to get her hands on that jerk, but she went above and beyond. If not for her, I never would've given Zoltan my blood in that basement to get him out of the feral state. I thought we needed magic for that. Didn't we have the mage help Astara and me?

You are magic, stupid, the snide voice in my head chirps but I ignore it.

I have no idea what I am.

Isn't that a bitch?

The fact that I would be dead right now if she hadn't given me her blood is not lost on me either. Yes, I felt the magic burst from me and knock Zoltan out, but I was way past the point of no return. My throat was ripped out enough that I would've bled out in no time. Not even accelerated healing would've come in handy. She did a lot of selfless things in a very short time. And none of them even said a thank you. They watched her leave as if it was a normal thing to do. I should've asked her about the book.

When the vehicle stops, I flutter my lashes and glance around, not even realizing my eyes are closed. Maybe now I can actually sleep for a week, or a year. The way everyone opens the doors at the same time kills that dream before it starts. Everyone is still too wired to let everything go.

I startle when the door on my side is yanked open, almost falling out of the car at Zoltan's feet. The look on his face sends a jolt through me and I do the only thing I can think of. Scrambling like a crab, I crawl to the opposite side and jump out next to Astara like the car seat is burning my ass.

Zoltan's chuckle pebbles my skin.

I scowl at him over the car.

"Leo should be …" Fenrir turns in a circle, "Ah, there he is."

Following the direction of his gaze, I see the shifter leaping out of another large SUV the Daywalkers use as transportation. I've seen them around the academy building too. I wonder if they take them across the portal or if they have a ton of them stashed here and in Sienna. I'll bet it's the latter. Astara tugs on my hand and I walk with her to the doors of the building. We are back at Zoltan's apartment. Because of course we are. No way will life give me a break.

"Does that salt thing work on demons, too?" I ask Astara just to erase the panic in my mind.

"What?" Her head jerks and she looks at me like I've lost my mind.

"You said demonic entities." I sound defensive but it's not like I've made it my mission to know everything about the different species.

All I need to know is if anyone needs removing. They can be whatever they want as long as they're not harming anyone … or trying to hurt me. My shoulders drop with that. I'm way out of my depth here. I have absolutely no idea about anything apart from fighting to stay alive. This night is quite an eye opener in the world of Francesca Drake. I must look dejected because Astara sighs and links her arm through mine as we stop in front of the elevators. I ignore the fact that Zoltan is right on my heels and almost tripping me as I walk.

"Demons are just like the rest of us, but not necessarily demonic entities." She jabs at the button to call the contraption to pick us up. "Roberti did a good job of keeping you clueless about our life. Kept you busy enough with stupid shit so you didn't poke around or ask questions." Warmth spreads through me that she's upset on my behalf.

I've been a shitty friend ever since Zoltan was taken.

Before that too, at least until she shouldered her way through the walls I built around myself.

"This has to do with the book, doesn't it?" My palms get clammy just from the thought. "Oh, for fuck's sake get off my ass." I elbow Zoltan when he literally looms so close his chest presses on my back. My elbow hurts like I smacked a brick wall and he doesn't even grunt. Jerk.

"The book?" Yes, I can feel his deep voice vibrating through my back because he doesn't move away. Actually, he steps closer.

I grind my teeth.

The doors slide open with a loud chime. I practically run for them only to realize I'm inside a tiny square box with no room to get away from him. Judging by that permanent smirk on his face, he knows I'm stuck too. Astara chortles while holding the doors open for the other two males and Zoltan crowds me in a corner. He steps so close I can feel his breath on the top of my head. My lips turn into a thin line and I clench my fists, debating if I should punch him in his pretty face … or the groin. The groin sounds like a good idea. His fingers snatch both my wrists like he's read my mind.

"You almost died tonight," he murmurs, but I know everyone can hear him since we are all in this stupid, tiny box. And like repeating that explains everything.

"I wasn't the only one, thank you very much." Lifting my chin in defiance, I glare at him. "So don't turn this on me by calling me reckless or whatever. You almost died too." Now that it seems we are deceptively safe, the fear of being too late comes at me with a vengeance.

I stab a finger in his chest.

"If you wouldn't have just let them take you, then none of this would've happened oh, mighty fucking Daywalker." Another jab of my finger between his pecks. "You could've stopped them, and don't you tell me I'm making shit up. I know you, Zoltan. No way anyone could've placed that dagger under your throat if you didn't let them." I get so worked up I shove at him with both hands. Not that it has any effect. "Why?" My voice is shrill in the closed space. "You put yourself and everyone else in danger you arrogant jerk." You can hear a pin drop at the silence around us. "Why did you do it?"

I deflate when the last question comes out in a pathetic sob. I have no idea why the hell I'm getting so emotional. It's not like me to show stupid weakness in front of people, even these four. My whole body is trembling and I hate it. As frustrated as I am at the vampire for pinning me in the corner, I'm also grateful he doesn't move when I tell him too. His hands are the only thing holding me up in this moment.

The chime is like a bullet going off in the quiet elevator.

Locking my knees so I can actually walk without wobbling like a drunk, I gasp in outrage when Zoltan scoops me in his arms. The fact that I can barely stand is not lost on me, but I still stiffen like an unbending board, my legs sticking straight out. It's childish and uncalled for, yet I can't help it. It cuffs at my pride, and I most definitely am not a female he needs to carry around as if I can't walk.

Zoltan is a male of many talents, so he doesn't even get frustrated at my behavior. He simply waits for the rest of them to exit and then, turning to the side, he walks out striding towards the door Fenrir is holding open for him. I'm still playing stiff as a board, my back muscles aching from being stretched as far as they'll go across his arms. The fucking Fae's head look like it may spin right off his neck because of the wide stretch of his mouth.

Sinking into the leather couch when I'm finally deposited on it, I have to rub my arms and legs to get the blood flowing again. Avoiding looking at any of them, I take a deep breath to continue the word vomit I started in the elevator. I have a lot to say to Zoltan, and all of it has been building inside my head while he was gone.

"I had to let them take me." His soft words are like a needle bursting my bubble. "We were getting nowhere trying to figure out what they were planning or who they've lured to their side." Zoltan is pacing but he still doesn't move away from me. He is doing it right in front of my legs, the fabric of his pants brushing my calves.

"A brilliant fucking idea." Huffing, I fold my arms over my chest. "How did that work out for you?"

"We now know what they are after." His blue eyes sparkle in anger when he looms over me. "The setback we inflicted on their numbers will give us time to prepare and end this once and for all."

"I don't mean to be a downer, but I must agree with Francesca." Fenrir is trying to get on my good side again and I know it. "There are other ways."

"The opportunity presented itself and I took it." Zoltan's large hand slices the air with finality. "Now we know."

"First of all, they turned you feral." I ignore Astara's

gasp and the blood draining from Fenrir and Leo's faces. Zoltan's eyes turn into slits. "Second, you don't even know what they tried to steal besides the fact that it's a book." If I look smug, that's because I feel smug right now.

"I was there with them." Is it possible for him to see me when his eyes are slanted so much they almost look like they're closed? "They thought I wouldn't be leaving that place alive, so they loved sharing what they were planning to do." Zoltan turns his head to look at Fenrir and Leo. One click glance at Astara shows she has gone as pale as a sheet and has a horrified look plastered on her face. "They are freeing the Titans. We will not let that happen."

"We secured the book they were after." Fenrir rubs his chin thoughtfully. "I'm not sure that will stop them for long but it's a start."

"I'll make sure the security around the academy is tight." Leo stands up from the chair he is sitting on, stretching his arms like a cat instead of a wolf for the second time tonight. I'm not sure it's smart to point that out right now. "I'm off, though. There is way too much to do."

"I'll come with you." Fenrir straightens and is already moving after the shifter, but he stops to give Astara a meaningful look. "We need to talk to Argoz. Take advantage of the time we are given."

"Yup." I jump up like I was sitting on needles. "We should go."

Astara doesn't say anything. She's still pale when she follows Fenrir, and it doesn't take long for him to tuck her under his arm to lead her out of the apartment. My feet can't move fast enough to catch up with them, but I play it cool so it doesn't look like I'm running away from the place. Just because I feel like I'm on the edge doesn't mean I love showing the vampire how he affects me.

Arms wrap around my middle and hoist my feet off the floor just as I reach the door. My wide eyes connect to Fenrir's and the Fae looks like he is gloating, a dumb smile lining his perfect face. But then the door closes and I'm locked inside with Zoltan. Alone.

My heart skips a beat.

Chapter Twenty-Two

"I'm sorry."

I almost swallow my tongue at Zoltan's whispered words when he tucks his head on my hair. With my heart hammering and bruising my ribcage, I'm too afraid to turn around and look at him. Although even if I want to, that isn't possible with me dangling in his arms the way I am...

"For what?" I have to clear my throat twice before I can speak without croaking.

"For putting you in the position to risk your life … for not making sure you knew what I was planning even before they attacked the portal." His words are muffled in my hair. "And for scaring you most of all."

"They brainwashed you, didn't they?" It's really stupid that I melt in his arms when he chuckles.

"It helped to set my priorities straight, I'd say." My stomach drops to the floor when he turns around, walking with a purpose in the direction of the bedroom I used to change.

"You're right. We should go look for Roberti and Alex."

I sound panicked and the words come out in a rush. I don't care. "No time like the present. It's a perfect priority to have."

My ribs will break if the galloping in my chest doesn't stop. Zoltan's dark chuckle sends spikes of adrenaline through me, but I hang limply unable to move. The damn door is getting too close and I can't even flail like I want to save my life. *This is a bad idea, Franky. A very, very bad idea.* Even the voice in my head sounds panicked.

"I have a lot to make up for," the vampire tells me as he opens the door of the bedroom, but he doesn't head for the bed.

The sigh is wrenched from the depths of my soul, but it chokes me halfway through when he strides inside the bathroom and plants my ass on the slab acting as a sink. Zoltan rubs his hands up and down my arms in a soothing manner but that doesn't help at all. My eyes are darting around in search of a way out. I'm also hyperventilating, so that might have something to do with him giving me time in case I'm about to faint. It's a great possibility at the moment.

"Look at me." He lifts my face with a finger crooked under my chin. "It's me, Francesca. Since when do you fear me?"

It takes a lot of blinking to bring his face into focus and for my brain to catch up with what he says. My stubborn side rears its ugly head at him implying that I'm afraid of him. Stupid arrogant males assuming they have anything to do with the way females react. I'm not scared of Zoltan or anyone else. I'm scared of myself because I'm stupid enough to let him inside my heart. *You already did.* Yup the snide voice is back, gloating at the sweaty mess I am right now.

"Just relax, please." Zoltan's lips press against my forehead and on the tip of my nose before moving from one eyelid to the other. "I'm not asking for anything from you. Just let me take care of you."

"I'm not scared of you." I finally find my voice but it sounds faint. "And I don't need anyone to take care of me." Wiggling to get down only makes his hip press closer between my legs so I stop.

"I didn't say you need it." My world tilts upside down when he kisses the life out of me. "I need it," he murmurs after leaning back a little bit.

Stunned and stupefied because he turns my brain to mush with the kiss, I let him pull me to my feet. My body slides down his firm chest before my feet find the cold tiles. With one hand gripping my arm to hold me steady, he turns around and yanks the shower door open, leaning in to fiddle with the taps. I jump out of my skin when the water gushes out of the showerhead, the glass fogging up fast from the steam.

This is all surreal to me. Yes, I've wanted Zoltan from the moment I set my eyes on him. But unless you are dead there is no way for anyone to stay indifferent to the vampire. His body and chiseled features aside, just his personality and the way he carries himself can melt your bones like butter. He is a male that knows what he wants and won't let anything stand in his way. So why am I here? A conquest? A curiosity? A notch on the post?

A pawn in a power play, the stupid voice chimes in.

Curling his fingers under the silk on my shoulders, he pulls the dress over my chest and down my hips. I stand frozen as I watch this powerful male kneel at my feet, and my chest tightens when he lifts his face to give me a boyish smile. My fingers tighten on my thighs, digging in the skin so he doesn't see them trembling. Hooking his thumbs on the sides of my panties, he drags them over my hips and down my legs slowly, his eyes following the path. Goosebumps erupt all over me just from his gaze on me. Heat builds in my lower belly as I stare at the top of his head.

I'm left with my jaw hanging unhinged when he springs up and peels his own tattered clothing off. Zoltan dressed will leave you drooling. Zoltan naked will leave you a blubbering mess with your tongue hanging out like a Neanderthal.

Like me right now.

Taking my hand, he leads me to the shower and I follow without protest, unable to stop ogling every dip and bump when his muscles bunch up with each movement. Stuttering slightly when the spray of water hits me in the face, I'm glad it actually snaps me out of it. What's worse is Zoltan has that smirk back because he knows exactly what I am doing. Or what he is doing to me … whatever the case may be.

Turning me around so the spray of water is pummeling my back, I stiffen when he reaches for me. I expect him to push me against the wall and pounce on me with no warning. His hand comes back with a bottle of shampoo and my face turns all shades of red. *Way to go, Franky. Just because you are depraved doesn't mean he is.*

I swallow thickly.

"Lean your head back." He tilts my face up and I close my eyes when the water soaks my hair, the weight of it tugging on my neck.

Zoltan's fingers glide through my wet hair, working up a lather. I sigh despite myself. It feels too good for my sake. Having my eyes closed with him standing close enough that his chest is brushing against mine and the tip of his cock keeps bumping my lower belly is much worse. My brain makes up all sorts of things I want to be doing right now.

"Turn around." Zoltan grumbles low in his throat, his voice deepening with a husky rasp.

"Bossy much?" I murmur under my breath, huffing like I'm put out by doing what he asks.

"A lot actually." He snickers and I find myself smiling like an idiot a second before I groan.

His large hands press on my shoulders, his strong fingers working out the knots between my shoulder blades. My chin hits my chest, my head hanging limply while another louder moan comes from my lips. I should stop making sounds, but it feels so good that not even being embarrassed or self-conscious can stop me. He works his way down my back then does the same with each leg, turning me into a quivering mess.

I almost protest stupidly when he spins us around to take my place, but when I blink the water out of my eyes to see him washing all the blood and grime still sticking to his skin hastily, I press my lips together. My thighs slide against each other and it has nothing to do with being in the shower. My eyes trace the tightening and stretching of the muscles on his back while he rubs his hair with deft fingers to remove the lingering shampoo on it. He turns so fast I take a step back when his smoldering gaze locks on mine.

"Oh, look. We are clean," I blurt out with a squeak. I want to slap my forehead at how dumb that sounded. "I mean we are done so we can go ..."

He shuts me up by crushing my mouth with his.

The moment his skin touches mine, I forget my own name and everything else that is about to come out of my mouth. Zoltan's tongue coerces me to open for him, and I grip his shoulder when he swirls it over the roof of my mouth. Fierce need has me yanking on his shoulders to bring him closer, but he stays unmoving and takes his time exploring with his lips and hands. The callouses on his fingers scrape over the skin on my arms and back, sending a delicious shiver through me.

Gathering me in his arms, he pulls me tight to his chest. I don't need any more encouragement than that. My legs lift to wrap around his narrow waist, pressing his thick erection between us. Zoltan groans, the vibration of it turning my nipples to pinpricks stabbing him in the chest. He leaves my mouth with a nip on my lower lip and starts kissing a burning path down my neck and collar bone. My fingers tangle in his hair and tug him further down where I want his mouth to be. Not even the arrogant male chuckle coming from him stops me from yanking on the strands. He started this, so he better be able to finish it.

Before I burst into flames or start begging.

My back arches off the wall and I cry out when he sucks one nipple in his mouth, the tips of his fangs scraping on it. Zoltan look up at me, his lips tilted at the corners as if noting my every reaction and gasp while his tongue is lashing the stiff peek. I claw at his shoulders, gyrating my hips in hopes he will accidently slide inside me if I just move a bit more. One hand grabs my ass cheek, tightening painfully to stop my writhing. Moving his head, he gives my other breast the same attention, somehow keeping me immobile while moaning pitifully.

"You are a cruel male." My gasp ends with a sigh.

"Is this what you want, Ms. Drake." He stretches his body, letting the tip of his cock graze my entrance. I dig my nails into the skin on his back, scratching and clawing for calling me that right now.

Zoltan grins but his eyes tell another story.

He is suffering from prolonging this is much as I am. Good. He deserves it.

"Zoltan." The threat in my voice only makes his blue orbs burn brighter in his half-lidded gaze.

We both moan low and long when he slides inside me one painfully slow inch at a time. I think I'm going to go insane by the time his hips connect to mine, but I feel so full with him in me that all I can do is cling to his shoulders. He doesn't move but kisses me leisurely, taking his sweet ass time. I'm desperate and I'll beg if I need to.

He pulls back just as slow, not releasing my mouth. With measured, controlled pumps of his hips, Zoltan takes me to the edge of the cliff only to pull me back again and again. My skin feels tighter with each thrust of his shaft bumping the mouth of my womb. Like we have an eternity to stay in this shower, he holds off my release as well as his own. From a distance, I hear myself begging him to put me out of my misery or just kill me now. Whichever comes first I don't care.

"Drink," he growls through clenched teeth, and it takes me a moment to see him pressing the column of his neck to my mouth.

My heart skips a beat before jackhammering my chest.

"Drink, Francesca." His hips slam into me with a punishing tempo, a lot faster now.

"I don't need it." I gasp out breathlessly, hanging by a thin thread to sanity.

"Drink." I can hear the stubborn tone in his deep voice and my fangs throb in my gums.

Throwing caution to the wind, I sink them in the skin of his neck, the potent blood adding to the explosion building inside me. It goes up a notch but is still just out of my reach. That's when I feel Zoltan's fangs sliding into my neck. His growl sounds feral when my blood gushes inside his mouth. Lights burst behind my closed eyelids. I convulse in his arms, my channel tightening around his shaft and sucking him in like I never want him out of my body. Zoltan swells inside me before hot spurs blanket my insides. He pumps his hips frantically, his fingers bruising my thighs. It feels like forever until I come down from the high of the orgasm and go limp in his arms.

Tears gather at the corners of my eyes when I realize what he did. I blink them away just as he slides his fangs out of my neck and I do the same. His tongue swirls gently over the punctures while I'm turning into a mess inside. Drinking from each other is what mates do when having sex. He can never be my mate, but he gave me this. A lump forms in my throat. Stupid vampire. I feel the wall I've built around my heart crack open and I want to scream my rage at him.

Zoltan tightens his arms around me, sighing contently with his cock still hard inside my body. I just had the best sex in my life and I want him again. Just as I thought. I'll never be able to have enough of him. I knew this was a bad idea. Regardless of that, I hug him close.

"We should go," I mumble after a long time.

"No take backs." He doesn't pull out of me, still keeping me pinned to the tiles. The now-cold water splashes both of us.

"What?" He can't possibly expect me to understand what he is saying right now.

"You and me." He searches my eyes with determination set in his jaw. "No take backs."

"There is no you and me, Zoltan." I cup his face while fighting the tears that want to come. "You are a pure blood, or did you forget?"

"There is a you and me, and I know very well what I

am." One side of his mouth kicks up to reveal the tip of a fang poking from under it. "And I know what you are, too."

"A dragon blood." My mouth twists in a grimace. "Like Soren."

"But Soren is not the same kind of Fae you are, is he?"

"Why are we having this conversation with your cock still inside me?" The magic jumps up at Zoltan's words and alarms blare in my head.

"Because you can't run away when I have you wrapped around me." Zoltan sounds like it's a very logical explanation.

I gape at him.

"Fine, I'll bite." My channel pulses, involuntarily tightening around him. He groans deep in his chest. "What Fae are we talking about?"

"You told me yourself you are from the Courtless Fae."

"I don't get your point."

"Rules do not apply to you, Francesca. You and Soren share the lineage of being dragon blood, yes." He peppers kisses over my face. "But you are more. I don't think anyone has come across a bloodline like yours." All humor leaves his face when he looks at me again. "That's why Roberti will go to any lengths to get his hands on you. He believes that not only will your blood help free the Titans, but he thinks it can control them too."

"Nothing can control Titians." My blood turns to ice.

"We don't know." With that, he pulls out of me and leads me out of the shower.

My mind is swirling so much it's making me dizzy. I know nothing about Courtless Fae, or anything else for that matter. If what Zoltan is saying is true, tonight was just a small setback for Roberti. Next time he will come prepared, and I'm not sure I'll get out of it so easy. I don't even want to think what he will do if he gets me like he did Zoltan. I'm not even aware that the vampire has dressed me or that we've left his apartment. Still holding my hand tightly, and with the book in his other hand, Zoltan leads me inside the portal.

And right into chaos.

Next in the Daywalker Series

vinci-books.com/initiated

The greatest currency in a war for power... is blood.

We delayed the end, not stopped it. Zoltan's return brings answers, but initiation into the Daywalkers' secret guild could kill me—and the sacrifice this time might be someone I can't afford to lose.

Turn the page for a free preview...

Initiated: Chapter One

"You have got to be kidding me!"

Snarling, my fangs drop from the freaking chaos in front of my eyes. Zoltan shoves me behind his back the second we step out of the portal, both of us ducking to avoid the blast of magic hurling through the air aimed at our heads. The wards of the portal prevent whatever spell is thrown from damaging our gateway to the human world sending sparks all over the place like some creepy fireworks show, burning like hell when it lands on my exposed skin. The frustrated growl coming out of Zoltan tells me he is not doing much better than me.

"What in the fates name is going on?"

My words come out shaky while I run to the line of trees in a half crouch, Zoltan yanking on my arm as he guides us there. From what I was able to see before my eyes bulged out of my skull, everyone in the academy is in the clearing surrounding the portal. You can't tell who is fighting whom, growls, snarls, and roars creating a constant hum around my head making me feel dizzy. The air is saturated with magic, tightening my skin while forcing my own power to swirl and pulse at the center of my chest. The only thing keeping me from losing my shit is the lack of white clothing that indicates hunters are in the middle of this clusterfuck.

A wolf comes out of the forest, snapping his head my way as he sails through the trees. He barely misses us. I jerk back and twist around, pulling Zoltan along with me at the last moment. The shifter lands gracefully on the ground but doesn't leave to join the fight like I expect him to. He also doesn't attack. The moon shines on his fur like liquid steel when he hunches down baring his sharp canines. Lifting his muzzle at the sky, he howls, and the sound raises goosebumps all over my arms and legs. It's a call, I just don't know what kind. Is it to announce his presence, to let his brethren know he's arrived? Or is it to tell them where we are? If it's the latter, Zoltan and I are about to fight for our lives … again. I see the vampire tucking the damn book he was holding at the small of his back, covering it with his shirt.

Answering calls echo through the night, and the short hairs on the back of my neck stand at attention when a deep growl followed by a hissing purr reaches my ears. Glancing up, I can't miss the panther poised on top of a thick branch above our heads, his legs bent as if ready to pounce. The quickening of my heartbeat is not lost on the feline, or on Zoltan. I clench my jaw but don't feel too bad about freaking out since the noise the panther makes is the same one a person may hear a second before their throat is ripped out. Sharp pain zips through my neck and shoulders. My head jerks up and I lock gazes with the predator. Green eyes like jewels glitter in the pinpricks of the moonlight, the large black body blending into the shadows like a ghost. My heart wrenches to the back of my throat and lodges there for a moment before I realize the shifter is not looking at me. His entire focus is aimed over our heads at the fighting that hasn't paused for a second with our arrival.

"What the fuck is happening here?" Zoltan's deep voice makes me jump out of my skin.

Being just inside the line of trees, the shadows give us enough cover not to be noticed. I watch the wolf step back to where we are standing, his eyes never leaving the battle. The panther drops next to me with barely a sound, nudging me further into the forest with his massive body. I'm clutching Zoltan's hand for dear life while my mind short-circuits, unable to form a coherent thought even if my life depends on it. Thank God it doesn't. The hoots of owls spread over our heads and mix with the cacophony of flesh hitting flesh. A grunt sends a crackle of magic rippling through our surroundings and the wolf transforms in front of our eyes. Rolling his neck with a loud crack, he lifts from his crouch, taking his full human form once more.

"The Board riled everyone that didn't join us in the human realm, feeding them stories that we are deflecting from the cause since we are following Drake. They were waiting for us when we got back." The snarl of his animal is clear in his growled words. "Leo made us walk through the portal in large groups, so thankfully we lost only a few before we could fight back."

"Who is feeding the Board these bullshit stories?" Relieved that we don't have to fight these two, I snatch his arm and make him to look at me. "Roberti and Alexius are here?"

"Drake." He thumps his fist over his heart, and mine stutters against my ribcage. "The Board was waiting, calling us traitors. I don't know if someone filled their heads with it, or if they did it on their own." His gray eyes turn on Zoltan and something passes between the two males—something that pisses me off.

"I see." The one word wonder is back and I glare at him.

"Oh, great!" I clap my hands like a two-year-old. "Good for you, bloodsucker. I, on the other hand, don't see shit." Zoltan's lips twitch and I want to slap the smirk off his pretty face. "Want to share?"

"You are a bloodsucker, too." Zoltan's blue eyes darken, the smoldering gaze reminding me of what happened in the shower not that long ago. Butterflies erupt in my lower belly, making me squirm.

"Half ..." Sounding breathless, I can't hide the damn reaction my body has to him.

His nostrils flare.

"The Board has the vampires and a good number of others on their side." The shifter clears his throat angling his body away from me to hide the jutting erection between his thighs.

Oh, great. Thanks to the jerk gloating at me, I'm throwing fuck me vibes like there is no tomorrow, at least if his growing smile is any indication. *Perfect timing Franky, like always.* My inner voice couldn't sound snarkier if it tried.

"All the vampires are backing them up?" Zoltan's voice is low and he doesn't take his eyes off me. A muscle jumps in his jaw.

"Not all. After Astara came through a good chunk have our back. Silas's son and his lackeys are still fighting and will never stray from what that old fool says." With great difficulty, I look away from the vamp just as the shifter frowns, his head tilting to the side as if he is trying to hear something. "Perfect, Leo is coming this way. I'll go help the others out."

With a sharp nod at Zoltan and another thump of his fist over his heart aimed at me, he shifts and bolts out of the trees. I hiss, startled when something brushes against my arm. The panther nudges me to the side and shoves his head under my hand. I forget the large cat is here and I have a predator as silent as death standing next to me. *This is why you'll die one of these days, for not paying attention.* The voice in my head reminds me of my shortcomings.

"Is this another of the plans you made without letting the rest of us know?" I round on Zoltan, and if I sound bitter, it's because I am.

I still haven't forgiven him for planning to be captured and giving that asshole Roberti the pleasure of turning him feral. The jerk can act tough and like he is invincible as much as he likes, but it doesn't change anything. He didn't know my blood could cure him. None of us knew, and if it wasn't for Myst—regardless how lacking her tactics were— we would've lost him. One of us would've had to kill him. The sight of Zoltan's red eyes burning with bloodlust and his beautiful face twisted in a snarl is seared into my retinas for eternity. My blood curdles just thinking about it. Seeing him flinch like I slapped him soothes me, but only just. Definitely not enough.

"I knew nothing of this ..." Zoltan's long fingers press on his forehead, rubbing it harshly as if trying to relieve a headache. "I suspected it might come down to it, I just hoped I was wrong."

Waving a hand in his face, I prompt him to keep talking, the fingers of my other hand scratching under the panther's jaw with a mind of their own. My insides vibrate from the deep, satisfied purr coming out of the shifter, who body checks me when I snatch my hand back. The panther's upper lip twitches into a snarl, his long teeth gleaming in the moonlight when the head twice the size of mine tilts up to display the displeasure. A line forms between Zoltan's brows and a thoughtful look crosses his face.

"Well?" Ignoring the jitters coursing through me, I shove the panther's head away and rub under his deadly jaw again. "What does that mean, Zoltan? I'm not planning to hide here like some sissy while they're trying to kill each other out there. Fighting the hunters is enough to keep all of us busy for a while without being at each other's throats."

"Those that were fighting by your side in the human world want to follow you, Francesca. You! Not the old simpletons that can't see anything other than their own noses." His eyes stay on the shifter for another long moment before turning his blue gaze on me. My lungs feel tight like there isn't enough air to inflate them when he says my name with that slightly unidentifiable accent of his. "The Board is not known to willingly share the power they have over everyone. You can't tell me it didn't cross your mind. You are too cunning not to have thought of it before."

Hell yes, I've thought of it. It's been drilling holes in my head since the night Roberti sent me into the gaping mouth of the hungry beast that is Daywalker Academy. I just stupidly thought that with the hunters almost decimating us twice that the old fools were more worried about keeping us alive. Keeping us still a secret to the humans, that should've made them more worried instead of how much influence they have over the rest of us. That pink tutu I threatened Soren with sounds more and more like a great possibility. He could've warned me if nothing else. A throbbing heart-beat starts at my temples, numbing my head.

"I wouldn't say cunning." Grinding my teeth, my nails

dig harder under the panther's chin and the asshole snaps his sharp jaw at me until I flinch away. "I'd say prepared so I can keep my head on my shoulders. Those like me need to have eyes in the back of our heads if we want to continue breathing. That's survival 101 in Sienna for you, pure blood. Not cunning." He narrows his eyes at me when I smile, more of a baring of teeth than anything else. I'm learning tricks from the shifter purring next to me real fast. "You and Fenrir on the other hand …" My shoulder jerks up in a shrug. "Can you say the same?"

"They can't."

Leo steps out from between two trees, luckily with sweats hanging low on his hips. His hair is sticking out every which way in tufts, five slashes are rapidly healing on the right side of his torso, and his left arm is twitching from the residual magic still sizzling on it where he's been hit by a spell.

"None of us can say that. That's why they want to follow you, Drake. You are not power hungry, and that's refreshing." A confused look flashes through Leo's green eyes when he looks at the panther glued to my side, but it's so fast I would've missed it if I wasn't staring at him. "Zoltan." He nods at the now-glaring vamp.

"How many did we lose?" Zoltan is all business now, whatever is bothering him now pushed aside, though I have no doubt I'll hear all about it later.

"None." Leo rubs the back of his neck, his eyebrows disappearing in his hairline. "They are not trying to kill us, just incapacitating before we get dragged to the lower levels." His cheeks puff out when he blows a deep breath. "I'm thinking someone has been feeding the Board bullshit and they are not sure who to believe. It's the only reason we are not getting maimed and killed. Unless …"

Him and Zoltan stare at each other, the sound of the fighting filling the space around us. Even the panther bristles along with me at the two males. All these unspoken, or half spoken things are fraying my nerves. More secrets, more puzzles and riddles that have proven to bring death and nothing else. The same shit Soren has been pulling since the day I met him.

I'm tired of it all.

"You three stay here. I'll be right back." I try to sidestep the panther, but the shifter only moves with me, as graceful as a dancer who is preventing me from leaving the cover of the trees. "Do you mind?"

Scowling at the damn animal, I knee it in the rump. His long tail flicks around, slapping my thigh like a whip. Yelping, I jump away from it when it comes the second time. Zoltan's feral growl causes the panther to crouch low, placing its long muscular body between me and the vamp as if the shifter is trying to protect me from him. My eyes dart around while I try to figure out how to best fight the cat if it attacks Zoltan. I freeze when I see Leo standing without worry and scratching his head in confusion.

"Don't just stand there." I snap at the wolf shifter. "What the fuck is wrong with this one? Is he going to attack?"

"If I didn't see him standing next to you while you were scratching him like a house pet a second ago, I would've said yes." The panther hisses at Leo menacingly, and my heart skips a beat from the sound. "But he is not joining the fight so he can protect you."

"Of course, he wants to protect me since he is a male." I hip check the damn cat out of my way. "I'm going to help the others. You can hide here until it's all clear."

I only manage to move about a couple of feet before a

heavy weight slams between my shoulders and pitches me forward. With just enough time to protect my face, my arms take the brunt of the impact when I faceplant on the forest floor. All the air exits my lungs with a loud oomph, twigs and sharp rocks digging into my skin. Hot air puffs the tiny hairs on the side of my face when the panther lowers those deadly teeth too close for comfort. His entire body is stretched on top of mine and leaves me gasping for air.

"I'd say he made his point." Zoltan sounds too amused and I vow silently that he is going to pay for this.

"It's not smart to go out there, Drake." Leo's bare feet come in my line of sight before he lowers on his haunches to peer down at me. "The Board is asking us to hand you over if we want them to stop attacking."

"Lovely," I gasp out, still fighting for air.

"They'll have to go through me first." My whole body turns cold at the promise of pain in Zoltan's voice.

Grab your copy…
vinci-books.com/initiated